AT THE CURB, Nikki beckoned and a long black limousine slid up before them. The sleek car gleamed outside. Inside it was a plush cave on wheels. Street sounds were muffled, the window glass was tinted and there were curtains to draw for even greater privacy. The seat was crushed feather and it was strewn with velvet-covered pillows.

Jennifer sank into the cloud-soft leather, the tips of her fingers stroking it. She took a deep breath of fur, burnished wood, fine leather and the faint accent of perfume—an inhalation of absolute luxury.

"Smells delightful, doesn't it? Like fresh coffee or chocolate," Nikki said. "It turns me on."

Jennifer smiled and tried to keep her eyes on Nikki's face, but—just as she couldn't deny the excitement rising within her—she couldn't prevent her gaze from traveling downward where Nikki's fur coat parted exposing a challenging amount of splendor thigh, and a shadowy triangle above it. To distract herself she reached out to stroke Nikki's coat.

"I've wanted one for years. I love the way the fur seems alive in the light, how soft and liquid it is."

"Soft and liquid, yes. You should feel it against your bare skin. *Extremely* sensuous . . . right now it's making me tingle all over. Look."

She pulled open her coat.

"You're not wearing anything at all!"

Nikki's voice was rough and smokey: "Touch me, Jennifer. . . ."

# JENNIFER AND NIKKI

D.M. PERKINS

BLUE MOON BOOKS
NEW YORK

*Jennifer and Nikki*
© 1982 by Richard Gellen & Company

Published by
Blue Moon Books
An Imprint of Avalon Publishing Group Incorporated
161 William St., 16th Floor
New York, NY 10038

First published 1982
First Blue Moon Books edition 2002

All rights reserved. No part of this book may be reproduced or transmitted in any form without written permission from the publisher, except by reviewers who may quote brief excerpts in connection with a review.

ISBN 1-56201-314-9

9 8 7 6 5 4 3 2 1

Printed in the United States of America
Distributed by Publishers Group West

# I

JENNIFER Sorel liked to spend (serendipitous) Sunday afternoons exploring Manhattan—not only its art galleries and antique shops, but its endless supply of photogenic faces. She liked to stroll slowly down Fifth Avenue in autumn, when the red and yellow leaves were falling in the park across the street. Sometimes Jennifer stopped in one of the great museums that command the avenue, but it was never long before she felt herself pulled out to the sidewalk again.

As she let herself drift in the metropolitan stream she searched people's faces and found stories in them. She was a successful photographer of great versatility and buoyant talent who had traveled many times around the world recording with her camera mountains at sunrise and oceans at sunset, world leaders and fashion models, student riots and designer jeans; but she was first and always a fascinated student of physiognomy. Faces in all forms and conditions of humanity were beautiful to her. She believed that through a camera lens a person's features were as readable as thumbprints—and that a good portrait was a view of the complex world behind them.

Many of the people Jennifer passed on the broad sidewalk returned her attention, for even in a city of heart-breakingly beautiful women she stood out like a flame in snow. Certainly part of the reason was her classic blondeness—she was tall and fair and blue-eyed and her shining golden hair swept over one side of her face—but it was also her smiling boldness, the appetite for life that sparkled in her wide eyes. She seemed surrounded by a glowing aura of enthusiasm and daring.

She was not demure. If a man caught her eye, the gaze she returned was steady and open, as frank as his own. Men who noticed first her hair or her eyes let their gaze wander over her tweed jacket and white sweater and down her gray culottes, looking for the soft outlines of her splendid body.

She looked exciting in clothes, but when she walked down the street in her hand-tooled boots there was something about her long velvet stride that promised she would look even better—radiantly, glowingly sensual, in fact—standing naked before a roaring fire. People of both sexes undressed her with their glances, and Jennifer accepted their tribute proudly, like a queen—flashing that dazzling Jennifer smile.

Striding down Fifth Avenue she passed hot dog vendors and dark Lebanese in gray sweat shirts roasting chestnuts, white Good Humor trucks, joggers in bright running suits, a troop of white-faced nuns in black habits, teenagers tooling along plugged into their Walkman connections, businessmen in three piece suits and backpacking tourists in huge boots, and to each she paid attention. Each face was a possible photograph.

At East Eighty-second Street she crossed the broad avenue and mounted the wide stone steps of the Metropolitan Museum. Groups of museum-goers rested there at the portals of culture, sitting in broken rows beneath the huge red and yellow banner announcements of current exhibits that brightened the facade of the great building. She squinted up into the azure October sky and sat on a step facing the sun. On the esplanade below her a wistful young man with a lustrous black beard sat playing Elizabethan airs on a lute. The sweet music rose liquidly against the background of traffic noise.

She took her Nikon from a leather shoulder bag, removed the lens cap, wiped the lens with a tissue, and put the camera to her eye. Panning the crowd around her, she looked for the dramatic features—a noble brow, hawk nose, flaring nostrils, sensual lips—that sometimes could be isolated in the lens of a camera. Parts of faces interested her, like pieces of a puzzle.

She saw a couple kissing on the steps above her and snapped her first picture of the day when she noticed how they had clasped hands, locking fingers as they lost themselves in a passionate embrace. Hers was a deeply romantic spirit—although she might not have taken the shot if she hadn't noticed the man's other hand on the girl's ample breast.

The second picture she took was of a soap opera star who had been recognised by a group of fans. Screwing on her telescopic lens, Jennifer got a shot of the flustered man holding a gold pencil above his head while an overweight matron crushed him in a bear hug. She wanted to capture the alarm on his face at the perilousness of celebrity.

Jennifer sympathized with him. She had not liked being on the other end of the camera—which was the position she found herself in when *New Man* magazine published her epic cover story on male sexuality. She didn't think that what she had written about men was all *that* controversial—not after Shere Hite—but it was her unorthodox methods of research that *New Man*'s giant publicity campaign had emphasized.

When people asked her about her methods her reply was always the same: "Now, how are you going to learn anything about a man's sexuality by taking his word for it on a questionnaire? That's just *his* side of the story of himself. No, if you really want to validate your information, you have to experience his sexuality. My findings are based on . . . intimate research. I challenge any woman to dispute them."

Now she was tired of all the fuss and eager to get on with her next project. But, she admitted to herself, it *was* a man's face that she searched for through the lens of her camera. She'd been fantasizing about men, their bodies and smells and husky voices, since she'd awakened in her Beekman Place apartment that morning, and she was in the mood to let herself be picked up if the right man made the right smooth moves. By studying the crowd through her camera she could select the most interesting faces from the passing blur of humanity. Chance was everything, of course. . . .

She scanned the sidewalk below, the people waiting for southbound buses, and blinked when she recognized one familiar ripple in a flood of strangers.

At first her eye was drawn to the diminutive figure because she was overdressed for the mild weather. She was enveloped from head to toe in a magnificent fur coat—a glossy sheared beaver with raccoon trim —that Jennifer fancied she herself might own one day. Jennifer's lens caressed the expensive fur, moving at last to its wearer's face. Although the high fur collar came up over ears and the tinted Porsche sunglasses she wore covered half her face, it was Nikki Armitage, all right. There was no mistaking the model's exotic, fragile look. A couple of years before she had appeared on the covers of two fashion glossies and a newsmagazine in the same month. Her image—softly vulnerable but possibly dangerous —was a feminine style that stuck in Jennifer's mind because it was the opposite of her own.

Then Nikki had quit modeling. She dropped out of sight. Jennifer had heard around the agencies and from other models that Nikki *may* have gone to India to visit a guru, something like that at least—which in the rarefied world of high fashion meant that she had dropped off the edge of the world.

She followed Nikki down the street through the lens of the camera and then decided that she couldn't let the opportunity to talk with her go by. She'd often day dreamed about using Nikki for a project she had in mind, but had somehow never gotten around to calling her agency.

On impulse, she stood up and followed the exotic woman in the wonderful coat down Fifth Avenue. But she didn't have to play detective after all, because Nikki jaywalked across the avenue and headed straight for the last available table on the terrace at the Stanhope. The elegant sidewalk cafe was filled with people having drinks as they watched the street.

The exotic-looking model was lighting a cigarette with a gold Dunhill lighter when Jennifer walked up to her table and paused, unsure how to begin.

"Excuse me," she said. "Can we talk? That is, I'd like to ask you something."

Nikki Armitage removed her rose-tinted sunglasses and tossed back her long black bangs. She looked up expectantly. Her eyes were almond-shaped, giving an Oriental cast to her face. Jennifer imagined that she saw a flicker of recognition in their black depths.

"Yes?"

"I'm a photographer," Jennifer explained, indicating the Nikon slung over her shoulder. "And I recognize you. You're a model, and I've wanted to photograph you for years. My name is Jennifer Sorel."

Nikki put her hand up and reached into a leather bag on the seat next to her. She pulled forth a copy of the current issue of *New Man* and held it up so that Jennifer could see the striking lay-out of her own cover article on male sexuality.

Jennifer laughed and stuck out her hand, which the small woman took and held in both of hers. Jennifer felt her intensity like a mild electric shock.

"You see, I know who you are, too. Please sit down. I thought I would have a cup of tea, but now I think I'll have a Bloody Mary. We must drink to chance encounters."

They ordered two Bloody Marys when a waiter appeared, and then sat studying each other across the table.

When she spoke, Jennifer's enthusiasm made her eyes bright.

"I've never forgotten how terrific you looked on the cover of that French magazine—what was its name?—a couple of years back. You know, you wore gold and silver, and there were all those gorgeous men in evening clothes in the background."

Nikki smiled almost shyly and returned the compliment in her low, husky voice. "And you are even prettier than your picture in the magazine. You are vivacious."

The stiffly discreet waiter arrived with their drinks, tall crimson creations topped with celery stalks. Jennifer sipped from hers without taking her eyes from Nikki.

"You said something very pleasing to me, Jennifer, remembering that cover. But I haven't worked in over a year, and I don't know that I want to any more. With your reputation, you can have your pick of the top models. Why do you want to photograph me?"

"It's what I call my visual intuition. Your look is unique. At least *I've* never seen it before. There's something . . . feline about you that the camera picks up. Something mysterious, perhaps even primitive."

"Yes, go on," Nikki said impatiently.

"Well, I would like to put you in the same space with some cats. I hope that doesn't sound crazy. It's all in my head: the lenses I would use, what you'd wear, the atmosphere. . . ."

Nikki shook her head. "I don't know what to say, Jennifer. Modeling doesn't interest me. I'm in a different part of my life now."

"Well, would you think about it?" Jennifer asked disappointedly. "I'd be very grateful if you would."

Nikki looked bemused. Her gaze was turned inward and the faint trace of a smile on her lips was enigmatic. Something was being worked out behind those impassive dark features. A coin was being tossed.

"No," she said at last, shaking her head decisively.

"No? But—"

"No, I don't have to think about it. I have a feeling about you, and I always go by my feelings."

Jennifer didn't try to hide her surprise. "Then you'll do it? Just like that?"

"I don't like to waste time agonizing over what I'm going to do next. When I read your article in *New Man* and saw those astonishing pictures you took I was curious about what kind of woman you were. Your attitude about researching the subject appealed to me. It even made me laugh. And now that we have met, I am thoroughly charmed by Jennifer Sorel."

Jennifer looked down at her drink. "Can we get together soon?"

"I'm free right now. Come to my place. The car is waiting."

# 2

AT the curb Nikki beckoned and a long black limousine slid up before them. A handsome black man in a conservative dark suit and white turtleneck got out and opened the rear door for them, closing it when they were seated in the dim interior. Jennifer looked out and saw him watching her admiringly.

The sleek car gleamed outside. Inside it was a plush cave on wheels. Street sounds were muffled, the window glass was tinted and there were curtains to draw for even greater privacy. The seat was crushed leather and it was strewn with velvet-covered down pillows. The floor had thick white carpeting, and there was a bar and a television set in the partition that separated them from the driver.

Nikki sat turned toward Jennifer with her brown legs crossed—a position which exposed a challenging amount of slender thigh. Jennifer turned her head to look out the window so it wouldn't seem that she was staring at the shadowy triangle that was exposed to her.

She sank back into the cloud-soft leather, the tips of her fingers stroking it. She took a deep breath of fur, burnished wood, fine leather and the faint scent of perfume—an inhalation of absolute limousine luxury.

"Smells good, doesn't it? Like fresh coffee or chocolate," Nikki said. "It turns me on. I get tingles everytime I ride in this car."

Jennifer smiled and tried to keep her eyes on Nikki's face, but—just as she couldn't deny the excitement rising in her—she couldn't prevent her gaze from traveling downward. To distract herself she reached out to stroke Nikki's coat, realizing too late what meaning might be assigned to this gesture.

"I can't keep my hands off it," she said with a tremor in her voice. "I've wanted one for years. I love the way the fur seems to be alive in the light, how soft and liquid it is."

"Soft and liquid, yes. You should feel it against your bare skin. *Extremely* sensuous—right now it's sparking electricity in my nipples. My nipples are very sensitive—look."

She pulled open her coat to show Jennifer her breasts. They were dark beauties tipped with nipples the color of blood.

Jennifer's fingers slipped to Nikki's satin-smooth bare skin when she opened her coat. "You're not wearing anything at all!" Jennifer said. The blood pounded in her temples.

"Oh, no. I never do. A coat is enough. The car is never far."

Jennifer's palm was pressed against Nikki's flat belly. When she looked into the woman's dark violet eyes she saw no bottom to their inky depths.

Nikki's voice was harsh, smoky. "Touch me, Jennifer. Pull the tips of my breasts with your fingers."

Her urgency was thrilling. Compelling.

Jennifer didn't need to be urged. "They're so *beautiful*," she exclaimed softly. Her hand moved up Nikki's chest to touch the dark stiff nipples, and then her fingers squeezed and tugged the crinkly tips. She was caressing Nikki's small, dark body beneath the opened coat, exploring the soft hair under her arms, the curve of her small plump bottom, the notch between her slim brown thighs.

She felt unsuccessfully for maidenhair. Nikki was bare as an egg. There was no nest of hair, only the ripe opening, the slick wetness between the soft folds of female flesh.

Nikki shut her eyes and threw her head back, pursing her lips as if in pain. Her breath hissed when Jennifer's index finger slipped inside her body. Her hips undulated on the crushed leather. Her legs quivered. She reached out to pull Jennifer to her, her small hands insinuating themselves under Jennifer's jacket and sweater to find her bare flesh.

Jennifer tingled from the tips of her toes all the way up her spine. Her breasts were swollen, aching for relief. She responded eagerly to Nikki's feather-soft stroking. The two women writhed against each other in the splendid privacy of the plush back seat.

She was terribly turned on, but she wondered if part of the reason was that she had awakened wanting to make love and had resisted masturbating to ease her erotic tension.

She was torn. She wanted Nikki badly, but she wished the soft exotic beauty had a sturdy penis smooth as worn silk between her slender thighs, and testicles she could roll in the palm of her hand.

When she broke away at last both of them were breathing rapidly through open mouths. Nikki looked sleepily savage, ready to pounce on the next orgasm. It was that look which Jennifer wanted to get on film.

"Play with me, Jennifer," she begged huskily. "Let yourself go and play a game with me. Will you?"

Strange as it seemed to her when she thought about it later, Jennifer didn't hesitate. She wanted Nikki.

"Yes. I trust you. I'll play."

"Good. Trust is the key. Now, I'm going to take you into my house and introduce you to my brother —but I want you to wear a blindfold."

"But why . . . ?"

"No questions, please. Just trust me."

# 3

Nikki pulled a long white silk scarf from the deep pocket of her fur coat, folded it, and quickly tied it around Jennifer's eyes.

Jennifer gasped, startled by the suddenness with which Nikki had begun to play her game. She was taken off guard and given no opportunity to have second thoughts about her agreement.

For the first time in her life since childhood she felt helpless, utterly dependent on another person.

"Just one thing, Nikki," she asked.

"Tell me."

"Don't let go of me. Once you start, don't stop touching me."

"I promise I won't. I'll stick like glue."

The car slowed to a smooth stop. Jennifer found herself straining to hear Nikki's quick, small breaths and then she heard the driver's door open and slam closed. "We're here," Nikki told her.

The door to the back seat opened and she was helped out of the car by Nikki and the chauffeur. They led her quickly across a wide sidewalk and up a flight of eight stone steps. A key turned in a lock and the chauffeur went back down the steps.

The heels of her boots clicked on parquet flooring and then they were climbing a long, curving staircase. Nikki held her arm and guided her down a carpeted hall. They stopped and another door was opened.

"When am I going to meet your brother?" Jennifer asked.

"He'll be here soon. John went for him. Meanwhile, you can get comfortable. I'll help you take off your boots."

They crossed the room in the direction of heat.

"A fireplace?"

"We like being warm. There's always a fire going in here."

She sat Jennifer on a plush sofa before the fireplace and knelt to pull off her boots. Her small taut breasts brushed against Jennifer's knee. She had removed her sheared beaver coat, as Jennifer discovered when her hands reached out and touched smooth fire-warmed flesh. Her blindfolded face tilted toward the other woman, who seemed to be standing above her.

Nikki's first kiss was as soft as a rose petal on Jennifer's lips. Her small mouth and juicy pointed tongue explored the inner red surface of Jennifer's bottom lip and sucked the pulpy sweetness there until Jennifer heard herself lightly moaning. *Like a cat,* she thought. Nikki was like a cat in the delicacy of her lovemaking.

Her hands caressed the small woman's shoulders and hair and slid slowly down her silky back to the soft swelling of her buttocks.

"I want to feel your bare skin against mine, Jennifer. These clothes of yours are driving me crazy. Let me help you out of them."

Jennifer slipped off her tweed jacket and Nikki's warm hands tugged the sweater from her waist and over her head, freeing her high, firm breasts to the air. Her nipples tingled and puckered and she wondered if Nikki was looking at them. She hoped so.

She unbuttoned her culottes and pulled them off her long legs, lying back in the plush velvet of the sofa with her knees slightly parted. Nikki's hands caressed the tender insides of her thighs, skirting the scalloped edges of her fleecy pubis. Her fingertips danced teasingly around the lips of Jennifer's sex.

"Oh, I wish I could see you," Jennifer cried at one point.

"Imagine me."

"Then let me hold you against me. If I can't see you at least let me feel you."

They lay sinuously naked like panthers on the sofa before the roaring fire, one sighted and one blindfolded, squirming and rubbing their breasts against each other, stroking the warm satiny curves.

With her eyes covered Jennifer felt a new freedom descend into her deepest sensual urges. It was as if her self-consciousness vanished along with her sight, and blindness equalled invisibility.

She squirmed deliciously and touched herself when Nikki's lips started to work their magic up her thighs. She shuddered with delight when Nikki's small, pointed tongue darted like a hummingbird in the cleft of her secret flesh.

"You devil!" Nikki whispered hotly. "You're so wet. It's like honey!"

She held Jennifer's trembling thighs in the air and pushed her tongue into the vortex of pleasure.

For a moment, Jennifer didn't know if she could bear the escalation of excitement. She clamped her thighs over Nikki's ears and rotated her bottom in a tight circle on the velvet of the sofa.

Her hands caressed her tormentor's body, tracing on the warm satin skin the grooves and mounds of the feminine landscape. She arched her back and thrashed from side to side, and then curled around seeking Nikki's own wet sex, first with her hands and then with her mouth.

Nikki growled low in her throat and Jennifer felt the fine downy hair on the back of her neck stand up. She saw the woman in her mind's eye with long black whiskers and tufts of ebony hair above her almond eyes—a slinky being of mystery and infinite sensuality. Thinking of the photos she wanted to take, she envisioned Nikki surrounded by cats—a growling beauty with impenetrable tawny eyes and a twitching tail.

Tasting Nikki called forth images of her tongue inside a wet rose. The warm honey rolled deliciously over her lips. The smell was clean and natural, delicate. Jennifer rubbed her cheek against the petals of the slickening flower, dipped and twisted her tongue in the tiny pink opening, and moved her lips slowly and ever-so-softly over the swollen clitoral hood. She knew how sensitive her own spot was to direct pressure, so she was gentle as she licked Nikki's naked cleft.

The darkness was a luxurious garment she wore. It was seductive, offering her senses unparalleled release. She could plumb her deepest yearnings about loving women without having to contrast her feelings for Nikki with her memory of the last man she'd been with. It offered her the opportunity to luxuriate in the senses left to her, to tongue and squeeze and rub Nikki's eroticized flesh without the limits of heterosexual imagery and its conventional responses that sight would activate in her.

No, this was no conditioned response pattern: everything was new, a challenge to her overwhelmed senses. She felt herself becoming so lost in the taste and smell of womanly arousal that she was disoriented. It didn't matter where she was or what she was doing—she was swept up in the totality of sex that transcends thought.

She pulled Nikki closer to her, hands around her hips, and Nikki returned the energy, rubbing her lips wetly between Jennifer's legs. And when they could force themselves no higher with the intoxication of sex, they collapsed in each other's arms and dozed off. . . .

A few minutes later she awoke to Nikki's kisses on her belly. She sucked in her breath when the other woman's tongue darted into her navel, sighed and parted her legs to welcome her.

Her disappointment was keen when, instead of pressing her soft body onto Jennifer's, Nikki broke contact. What was happening? Her hands moved up to the blindfold.

"Don't take it off. Not yet. Alain is here now."

Jennifer's hands dropped to her sides. She held her face up to the pop and crackle of the fire, feeling helpless and disturbed by the idea that a man she didn't know saw her in her aroused nakedness, but she could not see him. Her hands came up to cover the nipples of her large, firm breasts. She blushed.

She tossed her hair back, waiting for him to touch her, trembling like a deer in the woods. Her proud sense of freedom was being violated, but she stopped herself from ripping the blindfold away. Curiosity and desire overcame her apprehension.

She had hungered for a man. She waited for him to touch her. The smell of his excitement was pungent in her nostrils.

He began with her hair. She shivered; a chill went from the nape of her neck to her cocyx when he held it high in the air away from her head. She reached up to clasp his wrists, tugging his hands back to her body. He played with her breasts, making the nipples stand forth, at first squeezing them gently but then increasing the pressure so that she winced slightly despite the intense pleasure she felt.

She listened anxiously to the rhythm of his breathing, concentrating on him, trying to imagine what he looked like, what his hands were like. Would he be small, like Nikki? Would he be hairy? The heated imagination of her desire created different versions of him in glowing three-dimensional technicolor.

He didn't speak. He was master of the situation, this intimate drama, and he was enjoying his power over her. She was too turned on to protest: every nerve in her body was straining to anticipate his next move.

When his fingers brushed the downy lips of her tumid sex her slender thighs clamped over his wrist. His fingers knew what they wanted, knew the exact spots where she would be most responsive to gently increasing pressure. She rolled her hips and his hands stroked her delectable bottom, one finger moving boldly up and down the crease in between the half moons of flesh.

She reached out blindly for him and embraced air.

"Don't toy with me," she protested. "Let me touch you."

He moved closer and she felt the rough material of a jacket brushing against her. He was still fully dressed. At first it was like running her eager fingers up and down the rough outer walls of a bank, looking blindly for the night deposit drawer; then she reached up and touched his face and neck and found them smooth. She unbuttoned his shirt and slipped her hand inside over his heart. She smiled: it was beating fast for her.

Her hands dropped slowly down his front to his crotch. She rubbed the bulge beneath his zipper and felt an answering throbbing, as if a small animal were trapped inside.

It was frustrating not being able to see him. Curiosity built up within her. He was clothed, she was naked, and she didn't even know what he looked like. The urge was overpowering and this time she didn't resist it.

"I have to see you," she said, reaching up to pull off her blindfold.

# 4

A HUNDRED exploding flashbulbs bloomed before Jennifer's uncovered eyes. She blinked rapidly, but through her fluttering eyelashes all that she could see of Alain—who stood with his back to the fireplace, his youthful leonine head cocked upward—was the reddish yellow flame that licked lasciviously around the outlines of his body. His hands were jammed into the pockets of his black dinner jacket, hiding the long tapering fingers that had stroked her.

As her eyes adjusted to the light, her first dazzled impression of Alain was of radiant energy. The fire in his eyes glowed as hypnotically as the fire that leapt and flickered behind him. He made her think of an epigram of La Rochefoucauld's she'd learned in college French: "An ardent temperament is the imagination of bodies." He was a faun.

Although he was large and fair there was a delicacy to his handsome features in which Jennifer could see the family resemblance to Nikki. Their father's stamp was distinctive.

Where *was* Nikki? She looked slowly around her at the huge room. Dramatic shadows danced in the far corners of the high ceiling. The overstuffed sofa was an island, at the other end of which reclined Nikki, hands clasped behind her head like an odalisque. Outside the perimeter of firelight was a vast unknown, but on the sofa they were close and warm, safe and aroused.

"Please take off your clothes," Jennifer said to Alain.

"Not yet," he replied, his voice strong, certain of what he wanted next. He moved closer to her without taking his eyes from hers, and touched her soft blonde hair. She saw that his fly was open and shivered with anticipation. He stroked her, the tips of his fingers finding the soft hollow at the base of her skull. Then she caught his hand and took it between her palms as if to warm it, bending her head and taking his index finger into the warm wetness of her mouth. She felt an almost imperceptible movement in his body that betrayed his surprise, but she held him fast. If he insisted on keeping his clothes on as a demonstration of his masculine aloofness, she'd show him that there was more than one way to persuade a man to undress.

She moved her lips and tongue with zealous skill over his finger, pretending that it was his masculinity, while keeping her eyes—heavy-lidded with passion—on his face. She liked his thin, severe bottom lip and the full upper, how they parted slightly to reveal gleaming white teeth.

She was thrilled by the ardent gleam in his green eyes. It was a frankly lustful, roguish look—focused on a vision of pleasure he wanted to share with her, an ecstatic goal they would reach together with great gusto and mutual enjoyment.

She sighed delightedly when he lowered his head and brushed her lips with his, slipping his tongue into her soft open mouth. She felt dizzy and excited. His arms were strong around her and the rough material of his dinner jacket scratched her.

"Close your eyes," he demanded. The intensity of his desire made her tingle. Her knees felt weak. She squeezed her upper thighs together as she felt the warm stickiness start to seep from her.

She closed her eyes obediently, wondering what surprises he had in store for her. She welcomed the blackness a second time like an old friend. It freed her other senses—and after all, she could always peek.

He moved away from her and she felt Nikki's small delicate hands teasing her large rosy nipples, making them tighten into yearning tender buttons. Nikki's pointed tongue darted into her ear, licking the pink whorls urgently, her warm breath like a feather on Jennifer's neck. She found herself responding to Nikki's touch but thinking of Alain.

She wanted him so much she had to open her eyes.

He was unzipping himself very slowly. She watched, transfixed by the sight of his hand coaxing the thick long penis from its slumber in his trousers. He might have been opening a gift.

He caressed himself meditatively, as if weighing his manhood in the palm of his hand before awakening it—coaxing it to its full size with luxurious patience.

What a glorious sight, Jennifer exulted. Her hands moved sympathetically over her aching nipples. She licked her dry lips.

She held out her arms but he didn't move toward her. She felt a momentary twinge in her vanity. Men did not usually hesitate when she offered herself.

"He wants me to come to him," Nikki said from behind her. Her face brimmed over with sexual desire; Jennifer thought she looked drugged.

"He's your brother."

"Yes. I'm the lucky one. I know what he likes. Watch now, Jennifer. Watch this."

Jennifer sank unbelievingly into the soft refuge of the sofa, transfixed by the sight of Nikki on her knees before her brother, paying a brief homage to his majestic purple-veined scepter before reaching up to loosen his tie and unbutton his shirt. When he was at last undressed she knelt before him again and took his heavy penis inch by inch into her throat while cupping his testicles in her hands. Jennifer felt a stab of envy. When Nikki's stretched bottom lip brushed the pubic fur covering his testicles Jennifer felt her own throat go dry. Alain was trembling as if electricity ran through his arteries, but he didn't come, he wouldn't let himself go yet—as if he were putting on a show for Jennifer.

He lifted Nikki from her knees, pulling her up his body again. His large hands clasped the cheeks of her round bottom and pulled her legs around his waist. She clung to him with hands locked around his neck and ankles around his hips while he pumped himself into her. She looked like a child holding onto a tree in a tropical storm.

They were glowing red in the heat of the fire behind them, dancers intertwined in an erotic ballet, heads thrown back, mouths open, teeth clamped with the effort to rock into paradise.

Jennifer was so stimulated watching this spectacle that her hands moved between her legs to stifle the sensation there. It felt as if a small tongue licked at the entrance to her womb. In the back of her mind an admonitory finger pointed: *incest*. All she knew about the subject was what she'd read in the newspapers, and learned about Lord Byron's love life in her English Literature courses at Smith; society had forbidden it even among consenting adults.

She was more thrilled by the thought than shocked, she realized. Alain and Nikki were so beautiful together, after all. She resolved to look at incest —as it was happening before her eyes—with an open mind, and decide what she thought for herself.

The first thing she decided for herself was that the intimacy of growing up together had provided brother and sister with ample opportunity to rehearse the dance they now performed. They moved flawlessly, they flowed into each other. The second thing she decided was that *they* apparently were not conscious of breaking a taboo; there was no shame in their faces as they made love.

She desperately wanted to join them, but she was reluctant to interrupt. Nikki was shuddering now in orgasm, moaning rhythmically as Alain tensed his high arched buttocks and ground himself into her. Nikki's fingernails dug into his ass.

There was a soft sucking sound when Alain lifted Nikki from his glistening erection and carried her in his arms to the sofa, where he sat her next to Jennifer and then knelt between them. He kissed his sister's eyelids and ears and stroked her legs, which still trembled.

Jennifer waited patiently while Nikki recovered. She stroked her and felt her heart beating fast like a caged bird. She ran her fingers through the exotic

## Book Five

woman's wet black hair until at last she quieted and could speak without gasping.

"Did you see, Jennifer? My fantastic lover brother—did you see him?" She gazed fondly into Alain's liquid eyes and patted his cheek. "Stand up, Alain. Show my friend Jennifer what it looks like up close. I think she'd like that."

Alain rose before Jennifer. His penis was a proud horn between his legs. Its swollen head bobbed not six inches from her face. She wanted to taste it, and her mouth was wet and warm; but she stared up at him with a question.

"Why did you blindfold me?"

"That's part of the game. The theater of sex."

"I'm going to keep my eyes open this time."

He stepped closer to her and rubbed the tip of his erection—so velvety and sweet and yearning—over her flushed cheeks. She felt her throat tighten with excitement and nuzzled it in return. She stroked it with her fingertips, tongue wetting her lips as she prepared to take him in her mouth. To possess him at last.

She held his heavy testicles in her hands and felt them roll in her palm. She loved the silkiness of Alain's balls, loved stroking the perineum underneath them and on back to the moist crevice between his buttocks, where the muscular ring of his anus prevented her impudent finger from penetrating.

"I want more of you than your mouth," he told her, pulling away. "As soon as I saw you I was stiff in my trousers, I was bursting to have you. Don't think I'm being coarse."

So he knelt before her and spread her knees, pushing them apart so that he could bury his face like a hatchet between her thighs. She lay back on the sofa, overwhelmed by his urgency. His strong hands held her thighs. Helpless again.

*But oh how I love it,* she smiled to herself as she rolled her hips ecstatically and welcomed Nikki to her bosom, the feel of teeth on her swollen nipples. She loved being the filling in this erotic sandwich, the hot glue that connected brother to sister.

Alain's mouth was hot.

He radiated heat. His tongue probed delicately at her clitoris and then moved slowly up and down the glistening pink inner lips before plunging deep into her vagina. His tongue pulsed inside her like a flickering flame. She groaned despite herself. She writhed and her hands went to his head to try to control the combustion he was causing, but then he moved again and positioned himself so that the head of his throbbing penis brushed the damp pubic hair around her slit.

"Don't tease me," she pleaded. She had to have him inside her. She held the lips of her vulva apart for him and welcomed his aching stiffness inside the opening of her sex. She moaned disappointedly when he pulled it out, but he pushed it back in again, a little bit further inside her with each thrust, each time sinking himself deeper into her tight sheath.

He moved slowly with exquisite care and a sympathetic knowledge of where the wrinkles were in her vagina and how to smooth them out. He balanced himself on his hands so that there was no weight on her at all, and then he thrusted into her wet channel as if a demon was striking matches on his muscular buttocks.

She moved her head to kiss him but Nikki's mouth came in between them and her tongue darted past Jennifer's lips. It was a long, passionate kiss and when it was broken Alain kissed her. He sucked the sweet pulp of her mouth like ripe fruit.

Jennifer felt herself overwhelmed by an explosive lust she'd seldom felt before. She thought as

## Book Five

Alain continued to move inexorably in and out of her that she might explode—just go out of her mind and start screaming in one long wail of ecstasy.

Then she felt the first orgasm burst inside her. The sixteen that followed in rapid succession were her introduction to a new way of looking at sexual possibilities.

# 5

No one spoke. They lay sprawled together on the sofa, limbs entangled, dazed as if a comet had hurtled through the room and left in its wake the dying embers of the fire.

Jennifer rested languorously in Alain's arms, her leg thrust between Nikki's thighs. She stared into the glowing orange and red coals of the fire, watching it die down and flare back up in intermittent protest at its own demise. She was thinking that often after making love with strangers there was an unspoken tension, but she felt comfortable with Nikki and Alain, and at peace with herself.

Which didn't make it any easier to formulate the question in her mind. It took her a long time to work up her nerve to break the silence.

"There's something I have to ask you to explain."

"Explain what, darling?" Nikki purred.

"I have to be honest."

"I'd be disappointed if you weren't."

Jennifer saw brother and sister exchange puzzled glances.

"Well," Jennifer began. "You know that my frame of reference is pretty broad. You read my article in *New Man*, after all." It was awkward. She couldn't say it.

Nikki was no help. "Yes?" she asked blandly. "Go on."

"Well, he's . . . your *brother*."

Was that a mischievous twinkle in Nikki's eye? She couldn't be sure.

"No, he's my half-brother, to be correct." She paused and blinked dramatically. "But I still don't understand."

"Nikki, you made love to him! Most people call that incest."

Nikki waved her hand as if to brush aside convention.

"A word of two syllables that does not begin to describe the truth of our connection. It's a label that I don't want to wear, and I won't."

Jennifer appealed to Alain: "Do *you* see what I mean? That you live in a world with other people, and what they might think of your relationship can have a serious effect on your happiness?"

He touched her, palm flat on her naked belly. His reply was gently mocking.

"What evil did we commit, Jennifer? Did we hurt you?"

"Of course you didn't. *That*'s not what I'm saying. It's just, I guess, that my mind was blown."

"Just say that, then," Nikki said.

"We don't live in the world with other people, Jennifer. We're too rich to have to do that—so you see, our happiness is never affected negatively by other people."

"Only positively, like with you. When we add you to our world, we're happier," Nikki said cheerfully.

Alain stood up and stretched. "Making love gives me an appetite. I'm going to put some more wood on the fire and get dressed. Then I'm going to find John and see what he plans to do about dinner."

Jennifer almost asked him if she could take some pictures while he dressed before the fire. He was lithe and long-limbed, and he made putting his clothes on just as sexy as taking them off.

Then he stood looking down at them, resembling no one so much as a young English lord, unruffled, serene, as if he hadn't spent the last few hours making violent love with his small dark half-sister and a beautiful blonde stranger.

"You're so lovely lying together. No wonder pashas kept harems. You make it difficult for me to leave you."

"We're just going to relax for awhile," Nikki told him. "We're going to have a chat. Oh—don't forget John's going to Trinidad this week on vacation."

"Maybe I can get him to invite us along," Alain joked. Then he was gone.

"What an unusual man," Jennifer said.

"He still makes me shiver when he touches me."

"I didn't know when I decided to follow you on the street that this would become such . . . an adventure."

"But you've been all over the world," Nikki protested. "You are a beautiful, intelligent woman. Your experience must have taught you many things about love."

"But there's still a great deal I haven't been exposed to, or thought about."

"Like my relationship with Alain?"

Jennifer nodded. "I'm not naive, Nikki. It's just that I've never encountered this before. I didn't expect that it would be so seductive. I want to understand it, how it happened between you two."

"You mean you want me to tell you about unhappy childhoods and traumatic experiences?" She wrinkled her nose. "It was nothing like that. The truth is different."

"Would you tell me? I want to understand."

"I don't know where to start. Alain and I . . . we share a world. And we have since I was seven and he was ten, and that was twenty years ago."

"What happened twenty years ago? Not sex, surely."

"Oh no! It was just that we met then for the first time. We'd never set eyes on each other before that. Our mothers were quarreling, and Père Mitya was off in the Himalayas."

"Père Mitya?"

"Our father. His real name is Prince Mikhail Bakirtsheff, but everyone has always called him Père Mitya."

Jennifer remembered the man. There had been stories in the newsmagazines a few years back about a modern spiritual master, a Russian mystic who talked about the importance of sexuality as an available path to enlightenment for a select number of serious people. She remembered being interested in his ideas about the "science of sex."

"Why did your father bring you together after waiting so long?"

"I guess it just took him that long to get around

to it. Our father does things at his own pace. But then he called our mothers together and worked out an arrangement so that half the year we both lived with one, then half the year with the other. We shuttled between London and Hawaii. After the first month we didn't care who we lived with, as long as we could be together."

"Did you see your father often?"

"Not until we were old enough to understand his work."

Jennifer stroked Nikki's soft hair, touched her cheek. She wanted to hear more about the mysterious Père Mitya, but that could wait. Right now she was more interested in Alain and Nikki's relationship growing up together. There was something of the fairy tale about it. . . .

"When did you first realize that you felt closer to Alain than a sister was supposed to?"

"I really couldn't say exactly when it was. It happened so slowly, over such a long period of time. Even when I was very little, seven or eight, Alain would touch me. A kiss, a hug, a pat on the bottom. It was nice. Comforting. He liked to play with my hair. He'd brush it for hours."

"Did you touch him back?" Jennifer found herself charmed by this story. Her deeply romantic sense of how love develops enabled her to imagine the two young lovers, disguised in society as brother and sister, growing up with incredible opportunities for intimacy.

"Oh yes, I touched him. He encouraged me always, but it wasn't until I was about twelve that I asked him if I could touch his "lap"—I didn't want to use the vulgar words I'd learned in the street for his penis. I knew it was special, a part of him like his tongue, which was so delicious."

"And?"

"I was amazed when he let it out. It was like a little animal he'd put in his pocket to surprise me with. He used to say that. After a while I was always asking to pet it."

"He never forced you, never hurt you?"

"Why would he do that? He was my brother. I would have given him anything he asked."

She said this with such sincerity, and such clear, shining eyes, that Jennifer fell silent for a moment.

"It's quite a story. Give me a second to let the dust settle in my mind," she said. Nikki's lips brushed her forehead, breathed into her ear.

"Why do you call thoughts dust?"

"I try to think of my mind as transparent, like the lens of a camera. Unanswered questions create dust on the lens."

"Now you sound like my father. Perhaps you'll meet him one of these days."

"I'm sure she will, Nikki," Alain said from behind them. He stood looking down at them, holding small glasses of a red liquid out to them. "To stimulate the appetite," he said.

Jennifer sipped the tart red liquid. It was Punt Y Mes.

"Oh, do we have to put our clothes on, Alain?" Nikki pouted. The spoiled brat role was very becoming to her.

"John insists on certain standards. We agreed to abide by them, remember?"

"I know. Do what you like, but not in the street, and don't scare the horses."

He brought their clothes to the sofa and held the sheared beaver up for Nikki to step into.

"I'll have to change into something," she sighed with mock petulance. She wrapped the beautiful coat around her like a shimmering skin, pulling its collar up. "Something that John approves of. He absolutely hated that jumpsuit I wore last night. He didn't say anything, but I could just tell."

Jennifer was puzzled. "Wait a minute. Isn't John your driver? I mean, doesn't he work for you?"

"All will be made clear at dinner," Alain promised. "John Hamilton is not a servant. He's a phenomenon."

## 6

The dining room was an eighteenth-century jewel box. Thick carpeting, large mirrors set into oak-panelled walls, unlined red taffeta drapes on tall windows that looked out upon a small garden. Alain pushed a red plush *Louis Quinze* chair under her and she sat at a round table covered with a fine linen tablecloth. He sat across from her and reached for her hand; he was polished and elegant in his dinner jacket.

"Now, where's Nikki?" he asked, looking toward the door.

"She's freshening up. I should have gone with

her, I guess, but I like the smell of your skin clinging to me. And of course sex *always* smells delicious."

He winked at her and smiled charmingly, and his eyes went back to the door. It opened and Nikki walked in wearing a blue Mandarin tunic shot through with gold thread. Jennifer thought she looked almost somnambulistic.

Alain moved around the table to hold her chair, using the opportunity to stroke the backs of her arms as she sat down. She shivered.

"You gave me goosebumps," she said. "Do you think John will approve of this tunic?"

"I think he was with us when you bought it."

With impeccably dramatic timing, John Hamilton walked into the room just as evening was turning the gold light outside into silver. He struck a match and leaned over the table to light the candles.

Jennifer sucked in her breath. He was broad-shouldered and lean-hipped and he stood straight as a knife. His deep-set intelligent dark eyes and strong chin radiated authority. His lips curled just slightly with a shrewd private amusement, as if enjoying a joke on himself, for indeed he looked more like the Cambridge-educated leader of a Third World nation than a caretaker and factotum for two impulsive children. He wore a white turtleneck and a conservative dark suit, on the lapel of which twinkled a tiny silver pin.

"Good evening," he said, pouring the wine. With deft grace he served them cold lamb, fresh string beans, scalloped potatoes and a vintage sauterne.

Then, to Jennifer's amazement, when he had finished serving them he pulled up a fourth chair, produced a fourth place setting, and served himself. He sat down to eat with them.

If growing up in Greenwich, Connecticut had taught Jennifer nothing else, it had taught her not to bat an eyelash at the eccentricities of servants, but this was something new. The man refused to step into the background, to efface himself.

Sensing her puzzlement, Alain tried to explain.

"This is not in the usual run of things. John usually does not honor us with his company at dinner."

Nikki seconded this, adding, "I think he's curious about you."

Jennifer hadn't taken her eyes from John, who was browsing over his plate quite placidly. When he looked up his gaze locked hers. "I read your article. I thought you did a good job on a difficult subject." His pronunciation was precise, lilting, British spiced with West Indian. He paused and she spoke too quickly.

"Thank you," she said.

"I also thought that you'd barely scratched the surface," he continued, putting the corner of a dazzling white napkin to his carved lips as delicately as he had confounded her expectations.

Nikki laughed, a pure, silvery sound. "You see, Jennifer, John is our shepherd through the vicissitudes of life. He is a man of many roles. He plays the parts of secretary, driver, gourmet cook, wilful butler and game master in our lives—"

"And also," Alain interjected, "father, uncle, friend—"

"And lover. That too," Nikki asserted.

"Yes," Alain agreed casually. There was a silence during which John Hamilton poured more wine into their glasses. Jennifer thought she saw a wicked twinkle in his eye, but it might have been the candlelight. The corner of his mouth twitched.

She fished for more information. "It's an unusual relationship. . . ." She paused and looked around the table.

"We are unusual people. Our lifestyle fits our personalities, and John makes the way smooth for us," Alain said.

"In return, you understand," Nikki commented, "for a salary equal to what an oil company vice president receives."

John Hamilton chuckled. "And," he added, "frequent vacations. Don't forget them."

"So you see, Jennifer, John is unique. He chose to sit with us tonight because he's deserting us tomorrow, and flying down to Trinidad."

Their affection for John was genuine, and she saw that it gave him great pleasure when they teased him. Like a lion with cubs he feigned indifference, but his attention was close on them.

"Despite myself, I'm going to miss you two."

"Don't go."

"Oh, I must, my darlings. I truly must, I swear to you. My family has not seen me for six months. I miss my island."

"Who'll look after us?" Nikki asked in a put-on little girl's voice.

"Don't worry, I've arranged for a replacement who can do everything but cook—"

"—and get us out of trouble," Nikki reminded him crossly.

"You'll have to be on your best behavior."

Alain snapped his fingers—he had an idea.

"You know what I'm thinking, Nikki? Why don't we visit the house in Port-of-Spain while John takes his vacation? It's getting cold here, and it's so warm down there. . . . We could make love on the beach."

"Funny, the same thought had occurred to me." She giggled.

"That's what we'll do," Alain announced. "We'll open the beach house at Las Cuevas. John, cancel your replacement. We can look after ourselves on the island."

Nikki lifted her empty glass. "I'll drink to that. Will you pour, John?" Her voice was sweet, but her grin was triumphant.

John chuckled ruefully and poured. "There's no rest for the wicked, I guess. But I'm warning you, I won't take part in your escapades."

"Well then, it's settled," Alain said. "We go tomorrow morning."

Jennifer felt a twinge of disappointment that the friends she'd just made were going away so soon, but she covered her feelings. She had no right to expect anything from them.

She was stunned when Nikki said, "Of course Jennifer, you're coming with us."

Alain reached for her hand across the table. "Please come," he entreated her.

She blushed. "I don't know what to say. . . . I'd love to go with you, but I can't just pick up and go —not just like that."

"Of course you can. You're unmarried and you work for yourself. There's nothing to hold you here if you want to go."

"What would I be getting myself into?" She knew that she was going to say yes, that if she didn't go she'd regret it for the rest of her life.

"Come play with us, Jennifer!"

# 7

A FEW weeks later Jennifer got around to writing to her twin sister Marina, who lived in Southampton, New York. Jennifer's dramatically elegant handwriting leapt from the blue stationery.

> *Las Cuevas Bay*
> *Port-Of-Spain*
> *Trinidad*
> *November 18, 1981*
>
> *Dear Sis,*
> *I wish you were here because I'm having a*

*wonderful time and I would enjoy sharing it with you. You haven't heard from me because I've stolen away to paradise.*

*This is not the best season to be here, the natives say. Once a day there are torrential downpours, but they only last an hour or so and are fairly predictable. I like the weather here, anyway. I like rain—do you remember how I'd walk in the summer rain with my tongue stuck out to catch the drops when we were kids?*

*I've been feeling guilty for not writing you before this. I hope Sue McNiff called you with my message. I left very suddenly, I know. All I did was pack my camera bags and one suitcase and tell Sue to let everyone know I was okay, and that I was going on an impromptu working vacation.*

*I say that I'm working when most of the time I've spent here has been in the sun, but the truth is that I am working. I'm down here to fulfill a fantasy of long standing. Do you remember a model named Nikki Armitage? I met her on Fifth Avenue and one thing led to another, and she promised that she would pose for me with cats.*

*That's right, I said cats. Now all I have to do is find them. I've taken a lot of pictures, but nothing of Nikki so far. I spend my mornings driving around the island looking for felines, both wild and domestic. (So you see, I'm crazy as ever.)*

*Alain and Nikki have just walked in. I'll continue this later—*

*Jennifer:*

*Las Cuevas
Trinidad
November 18, 1981*

*Dear Marina—*

*I truly wish that you were here, so that I could introduce you to Alain and Nikki, and a magic Trinidadian prince who kind of looks after them.*

*I think I'm in love with all three of them. (No, I haven't lost my marbles.)*

*I'll tell you how it happened when I see you. Just believe me that I'm having the time of my life. I've become a new person—but don't ask me what that means. I'm still digesting this experience.*

*Don't be mystified. I can see you getting on the phone to call one of your girlfriends and ask them what they think I mean. Don't read this to anyone. I'd be mortified.*

*I know it sounds strange, but here I am, and I can't tell you how fascinated I am—the heat, the humidity, the jungle, the people (all nationalities, like a bazaar! Of course there's a black majority, but there are also East Indians in their saris, Moslems in fezzes, even Sikhs in turbans) and most of all, the sun.*

*Yesterday John took us to a place south of here called Siparia where we could look across a strait of water appropriately called the Serpent's Mouth and see the swelling green of Venezuela, and I realized that down here we're just a boat ride from South America.*

*You can see that I'm in love with the island, as well as the three people who brought me to it, but I know you'd rather hear about them. I haven't talked about them yet because it's so difficult to put what I'm feeling into words. Maybe*

*I should just send you the rolls of film I've been shooting.*

*Wait—Alain says we're going to a celebration in the jungle!*

*November 20, 1981*
*Tobago*

*Marina Dearest,*

*It's almost Thanksgiving, and since I won't be there to share it with you I'm going to try to finish this letter (at last!) and get it on a plane to what we laughingly call civilization down here.*

*"Down here" is now Tobago, the next island over: it's not as humid as Trinidad, and John Hamilton has brought us to a beach near Man of War Bay where we live in a cottage and frolic on the beach all day. (No, I haven't taken leave of my senses—it's the truth!)*

*The people who live here are blacks. They live in houses on stilts and they carve amazing works of art, which they stick anywhere. Their wisdom and sensitivity is impressive.*

*Okay, okay. Enough of the travelogue, you're saying. (I can hear you saying it.) You want to know what I'm doing with two men and a woman on a tropical island when it's approaching the Christmas season in Manhattan. Fair enough. I'll try to tell you. Maybe if I can put a few of the thoughts and feelings I've had lately down on paper, it will reassure you that I haven't really taken leave of my senses—although perhaps I've put them temporarily on the shelf. Maybe I can reassure myself in the process.*

*The most important thing I've learned from Nikki and Alain is how to act on impulse. I mean, I'd never really been able to do that until I met them. Everything had to be, you know, figured out and rehearsed ahead of time—from talking with friends to doing a major shoot. Now I just do what I feel like doing all the time. I can be spontaneous here.*

*What have I been doing besides making love? Watching fish when I snorkel. Lobster-catching on the reefs by moonlight. Going to visit Robinson Crusoe's Cave, near Pigeon Point in the south. Making love. And making love.*

*Let me tell you, a lifestyle of immediate gratification is very seductive. Nikki and Alain are used to doing anything that emerges from their fantasies, and it feels like I've been on a roller coaster ride ever since I walked up to Nikki at the Stanhope a month ago.*

*Their major domo is John Hamilton. He's a genie out of his own bottle—and he makes all this possible. This is his island, after all, and he's a king here. Anything that we want we get, but after a while down here you want so little. . . .*

*Right now Nikki is lying in a hammock sipping rum from a coconut Alain just cut for her. We're actually on the beach, there are fires going, people doing the limbo in the sand, smoking weed, getting loose—and loco—*

*How can I explain these seductive children to you? Alain is utterly self-propelled and seemingly uncontrolled, except by John Hamilton. I've never met anyone who takes maleness and sexuality into such different dimensions. Alain recognises no boundaries—that I've seen—which makes him a free man, and I've never met one before. He's spoiled, I think, but so brilliant it doesn't really matter.*

*Nikki, as you know, used to be a top model.*

*The major agencies—plural because she is temperamental—plastered her image all over the world. (She even ran into a tattered poster of herself holding up a soft drink in the local general store here.) Most of the time we're like sisters, but sometimes she throws me a curve. I'm fascinated by her quickness, her spontaneity. We were at a party on the beach last night. People roasted a pig and we all sat on the sand and drank a lot of rum. Then she was taken with this notion that she was Neptune's Daughter, the goddess of the waves.*

*She ran out into the surf, with Alain chasing her—naked, because he was having a heart-to-heart with a dusky native maiden when he heard that Nikki was feeling dramatic—and she swam far out into the ocean, with the bright moonlight making the choppy waves silvery. He leaped into the water and swam after her, and so did three other men! The quartet of saviors brought her to shore, laid her on the sand, and performed a vigorous sexual resuscitation that went well beyond mouth-to-mouth!*

*They were so turned on by her gesture that they had to get between her legs.*

*She's a little bitch, but I adore her. He's a selfish monster, (sometimes) but I adore him. John Hamilton is their keeper. I worship him.*

*John Hamilton is really the spirit of this island. He wouldn't describe it this way, but I'm sure he considers every tree that grows here to be his third cousins from another life. When he takes me around the island in his jeep I feel like a king's consort.*

*Anyway, I could go on and on but I think I'd better stop here. I hope all this rambling tells you something about my state of mind, but maybe what I'm experiencing is impossible to write down right now.*

*I'm all right and having a grand time and I'll be back in New York before long I guess. Right now I've surrendered to the Armitage impulsiveness. . . .*

*Got to go now. Alain says there's a place on the beach he wants to show me. I just hope it's a clever excuse to get us off alone. . . .*

*Kisses and much love,
J.*

# 8

A SULTRY breeze from the south, from Venezuela, blew in through the open windows of Jennifer's bedroom. She awakened from an afternoon nap with its spicy tropic smell in her nostrils and imagined that it had wafted over the Orinoco River Delta, which was not far away as the Bird of Paradise flies.

She felt refreshed. The rain had come during her nap but now the sun was out again and there was no reminder of moisture anywhere except on the leaves of a few tall palm trees. Somewhere in the wall of green foliage behind the cottage a keskidee bird sang over and over *"Qu'est-ce qu'il dit?"*

She pulled a lacy white chemise over her head and down over her high firm breasts and walked outside on the veranda. Hummingbirds darted through the air collecting the nectar of hundreds of ripe exotic flowers she didn't know the names of, flowers so lush and colorful and meaty and vulvular they might have been painted by Georgia O'Keefe.

It was a riotous sexual landscape that stimulated all her senses—her eyes were filled with color and light, her ears lulled by bird song and ocean roar, her nostrils flared to inhale the balmy scent-laden air.

The cottage sat on a low green bluff overlooking a white sand beach and the sparkling emerald smoothness of the Caribbean. The azure sky above was vast and nearly cloudless, like a mirror reflecting the calmness of the sea. It was late afternoon and the sun was moving down the sky.

She walked across the tile floor of the veranda to stand at the low stone parapet and gaze down on the beach and roiling white surf below, but she wasn't really looking at the scenery—she was thinking of the shooting she'd done that morning with Nikki.

She'd realized her dream: John Hamilton had found them an ideal spot for backgrounds, a waterfall with a number of caves. The cats had been tricky to deal with—a large lion cub, two jaguars and a leopard, plus some house cats, each of them handled by owners who tended to get in the way—but she had managed to get some spectacular shots. She had been right, of course, about the dramatic impact that resulted from juxtaposing Nikki with cats. She was sure that when she developed the film the viewer would be able to smell the wildness in the photographs, perhaps even be able to see Nikki's mystery as she saw it.

Unfortunately one of the cats—not one of the potentially dangerous ones, but a fat Siamese—had scratched Nikki's shoulder and raised a few drops of blood. Alain had been there to kiss the scratches. It was his overattentiveness to his sister that bothered Jennifer, that cast a shadow between her and them.

John Hamilton had suggested that they invite the cat owners to a party on the beach that evening, for on the island almost anything could be the occasion for a celebration.

She had to think about what to wear, but before returning to her bedroom she looked down at the beach again and her eye was caught by a familiar figure.

A woman was dancing in the sand, facing the incoming waves. She wore a flimsy halter over her large breasts and a long white diaphanous skirt low on her slightly rounded belly. It was Shairoon, a woman of the island who danced every afternoon in the same spot. Nikki told her that Shairoon hoped to entice John Hamilton to come out and make love to her.

Jennifer had followed Shairoon's attempts to seduce John Hamilton with steadily increasing sympathy. John was in and out of the house several times a day, but he had remained aloof, preferring to spend most of his time in Port-of-Spain with his family, just as he'd said he was going to do.

She went to the telescope that had been set up to look out to sea at passing boats and occasional whales. She fiddled with it until she had a clear focus on the dancer.

Shairoon danced like the magic spirit of the island.

She was beautiful and incredibly seductive; John Hamilton would have to be made of ice not to succumb sooner or later. She undulated like the ocean itself. Her large brown breasts spilled over the edges of her halter. Her graceful arms were raised above her head, exposing the soft black hair that grew under her arms, dark as the gleaming raven tresses that fell about her shoulders. Her smile was an enigmatic enticing one.

Then Shairoon unfastened her halter and let her heavy breasts fall softly free; they moved on her chest in a swaying motion. She stepped out of her skirt, too, moving her shoulders and hips so provocatively it was as if she were calling on the sea to come thrust its foamy beard between her thighs. Her hips rolled and her fingers spoke eloquently to the soft ocean air. She was Terpsichore incarnate, Jennifer thought, dancing on a deserted beach.

But wait: it wasn't deserted. Striding toward Shairoon from the direction of the house was a tall naked figure with well muscled shoulders and arms, flat chest, narrow waist, long legs and high buttocks. It was John Hamilton, come to claim his prize at long last. He was in a hurry.

Jennifer moved the telescope quickly back to Shairoon, just in time to see a look of stunned disbelief cross her face. That look changed to excited joy and then she was running up the beach toward him, her arms out, her big breasts bobbing. He caught her and whirled her around and around.

Jennifer's eyes widened when she saw John Hamilton's erect member. It was eight or nine inches long, black and slender like a baton. Shairoon guided it into the pink mouth between her legs, and then his hands cupped her ass, her legs were wrapped around his waist, and he thrust into her while standing knee-deep in the crashing surf.

Jennifer envied the ecstatic look on the woman's face, her gleaming smile of victory. She thought ruefully that her own persistence with Alain had gotten her nowhere. Whenever he made love to her his sister was a passionate third. They were never alone.

While she watched John Hamilton make love to

Shairoon she substituted images of herself and Alain for them, and her fingers stroked the button between her thighs. She slipped a rigid middle finger into the tight opening of her vagina and moved it swiftly in and out.

She was so absorbed in the spectacle on the beach and the pleasure she was giving herself that she didn't hear Alain, who came up behind her and put his arms around her waist, pushing his crotch into her behind. "You're very sexy when you play with yourself, you know. Feel how hard just seeing you has gotten me?" He whispered this into her ear, and his warm breath made her dizzy with wanting him.

She turned and put her arms around his neck. His mane of coppery hair and his mocking leonine features made him look like a satyr.

"I brought us drinks," he announced, pointing to two opened cocoanuts with straws stuck in them on a nearby table.

"Look, Alain. They're so beautiful, aren't they?" She pointed to the figures on the beach, and Alain peered through the telescope.

"It's like watching trees make love. So natural."

They sipped rum and coconut milk through straws and stood together on the afternoon veranda watching the torrid scene on the beach.

Watching aroused Jennifer, as it always did. When Alain put his arm around her waist she pressed her cheek into the hollow of his shoulder. His hand moved slowly to touch her breasts, but neither of them took their eyes from the beach. She welcomed the boldness of his fingers as they stroked first her belly and then her pubic bulge. She spread her thighs slightly to allow him to penetrate her with his strong index finger.

"*Ooohhhh,*" she moaned through slightly parted

lips. They stood swaying together like this cheek to cheek, stroking each other and watching the small naked figures below.

They didn't hear Nikki's footsteps behind them.

"Well, hello. Hey, have you two forgotten that we're having people over? They're starting to arrive, and they look ready to boogie."

Then she saw what Jennifer and Alain had been watching, and her eyes flashed with heat. Lust made her purse her lips and suck her breath through her teeth. "That's hot," she acknowledged. "No wonder you got carried away."

She moved away from them to greet the first of their guests to arrive.

*"Later—on the beach,"* Alain whispered to Jennifer before joining Nikki to greet the parade of laughing people. The women were sexy in short, gaily printed frocks and bright headbands in their shoulder-length straight black hair. They had shy smiles and high breasts, and their men were lean, hard and dark like cordwood. They wore tight brightly patterned pants and they had flashing white smiles. Their warmly lilting speech was a combination of English and a French patois.

Jennifer waved to them and ran back to her bedroom, leaving Alain and Nikki to greet guests; she had to get some clothes on. She brushed her hair standing naked before the mirror. Tonight had to be the night, she thought. Her belly was tight with desire and it felt like her insides were ready to fall out. Her rose nipples were dark with congested blood.

She returned to the veranda wearing a bandeau of white cotton around her breasts and white shorts so tight they cut into her golden thighs. It was almost evening and everyone was on the beach. The rippling, irresistible music called.

She walked barefoot down a sandy path lined

with saw tooth vegetation and approached a group of happy party-goers playing steel drums and dancing around a roaring driftwood beach fire.

Alain and Nikki were nowhere in sight, but a handsome young man with a bottle of rum asked her if she wanted a drink, and when she said yes he clambered agilely up a coconut tree to chop down a bunch with his razor sharp machete. He decapitated one of the gourds and poured too much rum into it, presenting it to her with a bow.

"My name is Henry," he told her pleasantly, reaching into his pants pocket for a cigar-sized marijuana cigarette.

"Smoke?" he asked, his voice warm as rough whiskey.

She accepted it, lit it and took a few tokes.

"Mmm, that tastes nice. From around here?"

"This stuff? Oh no, this stuff is Jamaican. *Ganja*. We're lucky to see it in this place, but John Hamilton, he's a traveling man. He goes everywhere with Mister Alain and Miss Nikki."

"I remember you, Henry. You're the one who brought the Siamese that scratched Nikki while we were shooting at the waterfall this morning."

"I'm sorry about that cat," Henry said.

Jennifer sipped her coco loco and felt the rum slipping into her bloodstream. The *ganja* was making her very mellow. Behind Henry the sun was sliding ostentatiously into an orange and purple melt. Sunset, and the evening air was warm and scented with the smells of exotic, fleshy flowers. The rhythmic melody of the steel drums near the bonfire could be heard faintly above the crash of the waves on the sand. It was a romantic evening, there was a full moon, and Jennifer was in the mood to cut loose, to let herself go.

Not, she had to admit, that she had been restraining herself. She had spent a month on Trinidad and Tobago and in that time she had gotten very little work done. Nikki and Alain made loafing so attractive that she was beginning to worry that if she didn't fly back to New York soon, she would end up staying in the Caribbean for the rest of her life.

And why not? A part of her could be tempted into settling into the easy rhythms of island life.

"You attract the moonlight in that white outfit," Henry said to her.

"And you're a shadow," she replied. "We're well matched—moonlight and shadow."

He grinned at her flirtatiousness and she stepped closer to him. Nikki was the last person she expected to see then.

Alain's sister walked up to them wearing a tiny black bikini that did not quite cover her ample breasts; the cups of the suit dropped forward, revealing dark spiky tips.

"Evening, Henry," she purred. "I see you've met our Jennifer."

"I was hoping to see you," he said to her. "I wanted to tell you that I'm sorry about the cat scratching you."

Nikki shrugged the small brown shoulder that had been scratched. "Then kiss it, Henry. Make it feel better."

Henry obliged by bending over her shoulder and licking delicately at the slight scratch with his long pink tongue.

"Alain was looking for you, Jennifer," Nikki said, wrapping her arms around Henry's neck. Henry licked his lips and winked apologetically at Jennifer. Perhaps later. . . .

She understood.

She looked down the beach for Alain. It would

be dusk soon, and their guests were beginning to shed their clothes. A man chased a laughing woman into the water and caught her in an embrace that made them sink to their knees in the frothy surf. When they rolled in the water they were covered with phosphorescence.

She walked across the beach to the fire. The roasting wild pig looked delicious. A woman named Mari who had helped her canvass the island looking for cats smiled and offered her a plate heaped with pastelles and vegetables—cassavas, eddoes, tannias. Jennifer sat down near the fire to eat.

The three men playing steel drums were indefatigable. Their arms rose and fell tirelessly, their heads were thrown back in abandonment to the music. People were dancing together, others were doing the limbo, and still others were walking hand in hand down the beach, or leaning up against the trunk of a tree exploring each other. She loved seeing the gentleness of the men and the trembling eagerness of the women. Perhaps here in Tobago sexual relationships were good because the men thought of themselves as kings and of their women as queens. They danced with gestures that were not learned on any disco floor: their supple dark bodies enacted everything from family history to personal fantasy, but courtship above all. Even their fingers revealed their erotic feelings.

When she had finished eating she licked her fingers and brought her paper plate to the fire. Then she walked into the warm surf and sat down in the wet sand to watch the waves roll in from distant European shores. She felt mystical faced with the eternal rolling grandeur of the ocean; her spirit was reassured by its continual roar and hiss. As if in primitive homage to the primal soup from which man had emerged, couples were making love all around her, their bodies covered by the warm Caribbean sea water.

Near her the couple she'd seen in the waves rolled joyously in the wet sand and Jennifer found herself staring somewhat enviously at her glistening pink slit and his cock, sturdy and thick.

When the moon came out, winking benignly on the tropical beach, Jennifer stood up and ran into the black water. She dived into the gentle phosphorescent waves and swam far out past the big rocks that guarded the beach. When she was tired she returned to shore and lay in the wet sand digging her toes into its graininess and letting the waves slosh over her sprawled nakedness—for she had left her shorts and top in the surging water.

Alain appeared, calling to her.

"You're a mermaid, Jennifer," he said, sitting next to her. "What are you thinking about?"

"I wanted to swim all the way to France and have a late dinner in a little town on the coast of Brittany."

"You shouldn't have gone out alone. Sometimes we get sharks here." He put his hand on her shoulder.

"I go swimming here every night. After you and Nikki go to sleep. It helps me to think."

"What do you think about?"

"It's time for me to get back to New York. Back to reality."

"Your work?" he asked in the uncomprehending voice of a man who'd never worked.

"Yes. I have the pictures of Nikki that I wanted. I'm afraid that if I stay around here any longer, I'll never leave."

"But what does your work mean, next to this?"

He indicated with open palms the paradise

around them. The full golden moon, the wide silver beach, the dark calm sea.

"Are you saying I should forget everything and stay here with you?"

"Why not? We'll travel. We'll do whatever we dream up."

She shook her head slowly. "You don't understand what my work means to me."

"That day you saw Nikki on the street and approached her—do you still think that photography was all that you had in mind?"

"What do you mean?"

"I think you were looking for something more than a picture. Maybe you wanted to confront life directly, instead of always through a camera lens."

"I have to go back, Alain. It's not just my work, it's my friends. My twin sister. My apartment. My *life*."

"I would like to meet your sister. Is she like you?"

"We're only a second or two apart in everything."

"Your rhythms are that close?"

"As close as yours and Nikki's."

He reached for her hand and she gave it to him. They sat for awhile looking out to sea.

"You can't ever quite surrender, can you?" he said after awhile. She knew what he meant, and moved closer, putting her head on his damp shoulder.

"It's a problem for me," she admitted. "I enjoy my career. My camera takes me everywhere, and I get to meet all kinds of people. I've always wanted to be a successful woman with more to do than please a man. And what happens? Here I am, and all I want to do is please you—isn't that crazy?" She laughed self-consciously. "And what's *really* crazy is that I don't even know you—that's true, cross my heart."

"Come on," he said to her. "Let's get away from here."

She held onto his hand and they plodded through the sand away from the ocean toward the forest. They mounted a low dune and entered a clump of tropical woods. There were Jacaranda trees and thorns and shadows, but where Alain indicated they might sit was green and smooth.

"It's a magic place," Jennifer said.

"It's one of Nikki's favorite spots."

"Oh." Her disappointment was plain.

"What's wrong? Don't you like it?" She could see in the bright moonlight that he was genuinely concerned. "Nikki calls this her enchanted spot."

"I can see why," she replied. She tried not to show her jealousy, but she wasn't good at disguising her feelings. It had never been necessary before.

"Don't be jealous of Nikki. She's my sister."

"She's your lover, too. That makes things confusing."

"She thinks of you as a sister."

"I think of her that way too—and then I remember she's also my rival."

"Rival?"

She nodded. "And stiff competition at that. You're hypnotized by her, and I like a man's full attention."

"You have my complete attention right now."

She took a deep breath and released it slowly. She'd said what was necessary for her to say; the rest was up to him. She could relax now and enjoy having him to herself.

"I know," she replied. "It's wonderful."

He rose on his knees above her. "I want to make love to you."

"Can you forget your sister?"

"I can."

*Book Five* 63

"Then fuck me. With all your heart. Give me everything."

"The first time was the best so far. Your eyes were covered, remember?"

"Fuck me now, with open eyes."

"Yes, I want you."

"Look at me then."

She looked into his eyes and saw lust glowing there like a promise; but she sensed there was something more that he wanted from her.

Whatever it was, she was ready to give it to him.

He was overcome with desire and threw himself upon her, surprising them both with his intensity, but she welcomed his onslaught: she had him to herself at last. She wanted to glue herself to him, to press her skin against his and feel his heart beat against the fragile wall of her chest as they lay together in the darkness. Her arms ached with the suppressed urge to crush him to her, as if they could be merged.

His hard flesh slipped inside her like a sword into its sheath. She held her legs up for his entrance, welcoming the strength of his thrusts, the slapping sound as his flesh crashed into hers, his thighs against her buttocks.

He gasped above her, grunting softly, pumping himself into her receptive body with the energy of two men. It was his enthusiasm that shot sparks into her soul. He was a storm between her legs and she pulled him toward her with all the strength she could summon. His penis was jamming into the opening of her womb, banging softly against her insides. He was trying to climb inside her.

In response, she tried to turn herself inside out for him, using her pubic muscles to make her sheath as tight as her mouth would be on his flesh. She rolled with him as if they were waves playing together.

At last he slowed and then stopped, resting his cheek on her shoulder, his breath coming fast. She held him and something moved in her heart. Something that had been firmly anchored drifted loose. She knew she was in danger of falling in love.

"I want your ass," he murmured into her ear. "I want you to give me everything."

"It's yours, Alain," she whispered. "Anything you want. Take me where you want to go."

"You'll hold nothing back?"

"Just be gentle. I don't like to be treated roughly."

"But I was battering you!"

"That was strong, not rough."

She could feel his pleasure swelling inside her because of her surrender. He withdrew slowly, feeling her sex grip him like a rubber glove that had to be peeled off. She cried out in disappointment at being left unfilled, but she knew what he wanted. His urgency was exciting.

"Help me," he hissed. "I've got to get back inside you."

She knelt in the grass with her bottom up in the air, resting her weight on her forearms, but she didn't like the position. She preferred being face to face, able to see him and the swelling of pleasure in his eyes. She lay down on her back again.

"Help me," he entreated her again.

"It's been a long time," she answered. "I want to, but I think we need some lubrication. . . ."

It was all she had to say. He cupped the cheeks of her ass in his hand and separated them eagerly, his mouth descending to the tiny puckered target. His tongue-tip penetrated the resistant ring of muscle and his saliva moistened the opening until it was so slick he could insert his little finger.

Jennifer trembled. Despite her arousal, she felt tense. She tried to relax herself muscle by muscle, but she was apprehensive. Anal intercourse was so much more intimate than the other forms of sex.

She held her buttocks apart for him and raised her legs. She felt the tip of his throbbing manhood push into her and she winced, biting her lip. She was well lubricated so the pain was bearable, but it was hard to imagine that it would be transformed into pleasure.

He eased himself into her carefully and slowly, acutely conscious of the tightness of her rectum as it squeezed his unbearably swollen penis.

Then he was all the way inside her, buried in her bottom up to his pubic hair.

"Ohhh, that's *so* good, Jennifer. Hold on, I'm going to move now. . . ."

She loved watching his face, distorted and flushed dark with passion, his bared teeth, bulging eyes, and flared nostrils—knowing that she was the cause of such intense pleasure.

His hips moved faster; he was plunging into her rectum, and pain had become discomfort and then a swelling as if her insides might drop out. She gasped at first with the shock of his thrusts, but it wasn't long before she was gasping for joy. She didn't know when it happened, but suddenly pleasure was rising in waves from the erotic center of her being and she was transported. Her hands caressed his flat chest and hard nipples and went between their bellies to snake a finger in her neglected vagina. She moved the finger in and out as Alain moved in and out of her ass and she could feel his hardness through the flexible wall between cunt and ass.

They were both out of their minds, crying and grunting as they rode the high surf of pleasure to the shore.

"It's now, Jenny! Stay with me. Hold on tight!"

She almost screamed when she felt the hot jets splash her insides; they were moving inside each other's skins.

"I love you!" he growled fiercely in her ear.

It brought on her own orgasm, so strong a flood that she had no strength to scream, but could only whimper that she loved him too.

# 9

THE 727 that carried Jennifer from the Caribbean to New York passed through some cottony cumulus clouds and emerged upon a scene that always made her heart beat faster. Below them many thousands of feet was New York Harbor, its whitecaps and swirls. Beyond it was the promised land, Jennifer's home. Xanadu.

The sun was rising over Manhattan when they came within sight of the soaring granite towers of the city. High up the December sky was crisp cold blue, but lower, over the Empire State Building, it was dusty orange divided by crimson shafts. Jennifer pressed her nose to the window and looked down on the island imagining that she could see her block on Beekman Place next to the East River, and her apartment waiting for her.

A chance encounter had taken her to the Caribbean, and now she was returning to New York—and reality—with forty rolls of some of the best work she'd ever done.

She knew that the photographs would be good. Nikki with the cats. The jungle. The cottage on the beach. Shairoon. The all-pervasive sensuality. She had her memories and her film trophies and now she could get on with her life.

She should have been happy.

In fact, she thought seriously about taking the next plane out of J.F.K. back to the island because she thought she might have fallen in love there.

Her ass hurt wonderfully, like a sore spot in the mouth you caress with your tongue-tip. Love was sitting on the tip of a pin, she thought wryly, adjusting her bottom for greater comfort in the seat.

She'd had a shower and fixed herself an omelet and rolled a joint from a small stash of Colombian that she touched only once a month when she had to puzzle something out, and then she poured herself brandy in a snifter. Cupping it in her palm she strode through her dark living room on bare feet and stood looking out at the East River. The morning sun glinted off the water. She watched a tugboat belching smoke.

It felt unreal being back in New York after her adventure. She'd met Nikki on a Sunday, a bright Sunday, and now it was a bright sunny Monday, only a month later.

But the month seemed like a year. Her head was

turned around. She opened the blinds and her living room was illuminated.

Blinking in the light, she touched a button on her telephone console that automatically dialed Sue McNiff's private office line. Because of her disorientation, she wanted to plug into the reality around her. She was pleased when she heard Sue's hoarse voice. Her cough was familiar and endearing.

"Hello. You have reached the McNiff agency, but Sue is out—"

"Sue, it's Jennifer."

"Hang on, let me stop coughing."

Jennifer held the phone away from her ear while Sue McNiff barked in a strangled kind of greeting.

"Jenny, what have you got?"

"Forty rolls of Tri-X. Sue, I have brought back a dream on film."

"Good. Now, how are you?"

It was always this way in her dialogues with Sue: business first, then the rough personal inquiry, the solicitous touch.

"Perplexed." She wished she could leave it at that.

"What the hell does that mean? You wanted to get this Nikki Armitage on film and you did. No reason I can see to be perplexed. Jenny, we can talk straight. You don't have to hold back with me. Aren't you glad to be home?"

"I should have stayed there. He asked me to."

"You mean this Alain guy?"

"Sue, he makes me want to do things I haven't done ever—you don't know what it's like to see beyond the perimeter through the eyes of a man who might take you there."

"Beyond?"

"Outer space. Sue, I know it's hard to understand, but it happened with Alain, it really happened. I wanted to go all the way with him."

"So *what* happened?"

"Nikki was always there."

"So what? She's his sister."

"His lover, too."

"C'mon!"

"Um-hmn. They sleep in the same bed. Have for years."

There was a little gasp on the other end; Sue never bothered to hide her midwestern innocence—especially not after she'd learned how to use it to lull others into underestimating her sharpness. She recovered quickly.

"Well, *that*'s interesting," she said. "Material for that diary of yours. But *incest*? Really, Jen."

"You don't understand. . . ."

"I know—you don't feel like going into it."

"Right. I want to know what I've missed. I feel like I've been away for years—bring me up to date."

Sue chuckled. "Well—this is just off the top of my head, mind you—but you had about three hundred phone calls. You're very hot, my darling. Verryverrrry. *Time, Vogue, Self*—they'll all pay fifty percent more than they would have before your appearance in *New Man*."

"Sex," Jennifer said.

"At this moment, you're the only woman around who's talking about the subject. That, and your photographs, make you an authority, I guess."

"I *would* like to get back to work as soon as possible."

"I told them all to call back next week if they were serious. I like everyone to have time to think about a deal."

"No one should leave the room unhappy," Jennifer said, repeating Sue's personal motto.

"That's right. You want work? I'll keep you busy. There's a couple of jobs you should be doing that'll take your mind off everything, including Caribbean islands."

"Tell me."

"I'll just say two words—Russian names—but only if you're sitting down."

"I'm sitting down counting tugboats."

"Yuri Muscovy."

"Huh? What about him?" Jennifer sat up straight in her chair.

"He wants you to do a portrait of him."

"But why? He's a dream, but. . . ."

"Fortune has smiled on you. I asked his agent why he wanted you, and he said it was because he'd watched you taking shots of his friend Nureyev. He liked the fact that you wore a skirt, and seemed so feminine."

"Oh no, all the wrong reasons."

"You wear skirts, Jenny."

"When it's warm, skirts are cool."

"Shall I tell his office to forget it?"

"Don't be silly!"

"You're sure you don't have too much on your mind? Emotional pressures?"

"Stop it, Sue. If anything can take my mind off Trinidad and Nikki and Alain, it's taking a picture of Yuri Muscovy."

Sue chuckled. "I'm glad you're back in town, Jenny. This job is not the same without you to talk to. The ladies whose beauty and grace keep me in groceries are barely capable of tying their own shoelaces."

"Call me, Sue, and tell me when I can see Yuri Muscovy. Call me right away."

* * *

Jennifer propped her feet up against the glass sliding doors to her tiny balcony and finished her brandy. The sun glinted off the decks of a Circle Line boat.

She picked up the phone again to call her sister Marina in Southampton.

It rang on the other end for a long time before a breathless Marina said "Hello" at last.

"Hi, Rina. I'm back."

"Jenny! Thank God, now I can breathe easier. I worried every day about how you were getting along in the forbidding Caribbean. The sun, the bugs. . . ."

"Oh shut up, Rina."

"I got your letter. It sounded serious."

"Forget the letter. I did something on impulse, and I still don't know what to think about it."

"Don't be complex, Jen. In the immortal words of Charo, there's eating and coochie-coochie. So how was. . . ."

"The coochie-coochie was fine, Marina. Just fine."

"And Alain?"

"What about him?"

"I was hoping that you might be able to say that you would introduce him to me over cocktails in the Palm Court. Something old-fashioned and discreet, considering the circumstances."

"Marina, just stop it. Stop it this minute."

"What did I say?"

"This is serious, Marina. Alain means a lot to me."

She could imagine Marina on the other end, adjusting herself for a long spell of sympathetic listening. With Marina's help she had always been able to set a straight emotional course.

"What's going on then? Just spill it."

# Book Five

"I think he might be the real thing, but he comes as part of a team."

"You can't convince him to leave his sister on a desert island someplace?"

"No. He's absolutely devoted."

"Then you have to cut him loose. Right?"

"It's not that simple—he sticks in my mind. I hear his voice right before I think I'm going to go to sleep to forget about him."

"You poor dear. You *do* need distraction. You could come out here, but I don't think you'd want to see Jack at this point. He's being a perfect bastard to me."

"I'm sorry to hear—"

"No, don't. I'm learning how other people feel. I've always been so lucky in love I guess it's time I paid some dues. Jack August is one of a kind. You knew what you were doing when you left him to me."

Jennifer chuckled and hoped Marina didn't hear. Jack August was the publisher of *New Man* magazine, and once upon a time not long before had occupied a high place in Jennifer's regard. But when it became apparent that he could not be content even with both the Sorel twins on his lap, Jennifer had abandoned the field.

"By the way," Marina said. "The man has invited us to a New Year's weekend at his country house in Vermont. He asked if I thought you would come and I said no. Was I right?"

"I'd like to go, actually. I want to talk to him about something. An idea."

A few hours later she was soaking in a bubble bath when Sue McNiff called.

"It's all arranged," she said.

"What's arranged?"

"Yuri Muscovy, darling. You see him tomorrow."

# 10

Yuri Muscovy was a god of Dance, both critically and popularly acclaimed as the most exciting dancer to flee Mother Russia since Baryshnikov had done his *grand jeté* from the stage of the Kirov Ballet right over the Iron Curtain.

Jennifer had seen him dance twice in New York and many times on television in her dorm at Smith, where she had been a leading member of an *ad hoc* Yuri Muscovy fan club. To her he seemed to fly across the stage like a macho Peter Pan, creating graceful shimmering beauty with a masculine body as perfect as a Greek god's.

*Book Five* 75

What Jennifer enjoyed most about her growing reputation as a photographer who could excel at any project that excited her was the opportunity it provided to meet some of her personal heroes—people she'd been dying to meet for years, like Yuri Muscovy.

He had a suite at the Hotel St. Etienne on Fifth Avenue. She loaded a Checker cab with the equipment she would need for the shooting and the driver took Seventy-ninth Street through the Park. It was right before Christmas and the snow was deep where people and their dogs had not flattened it. The trees were bare and black against the metallic winter sky.

She looked forward to meeting Yuri Muscovy with more than professional eagerness. She was a fan—she'd fantasized about him. She'd often thought, while watching him dance, that there were photographs of him that she alone could take. Some people sing in the shower; Jennifer sometimes began the day by dancing naked about her apartment to "Swan Lake."

Two bellhops helped her haul her equipment up to the penthouse suite where she was to meet Yuri Muscovy at noon. They accepted a large tip and left her surrounded by her bags before his door.

Before knocking, she glanced at her Rolex and noted that she was five minutes late. She believed in punctuality.

Knowing that Yuri liked women who dressed in feminine clothing, she had worn her three-piece winter white silk suit. The puff-shouldered jacket, gold-belted dirndl and camisole made her feel slightly overdressed, so she'd compensated by wearing a lacy garter belt and stockings, but no panties. Her motto when she got to meet a heartthrob was: Be Prepared. You never know.

She knocked again and waited. Presently she

heard footsteps and the door was flung open. She flushed like a nervous schoolgirl.

Yuri Muscovy stood before her clad in black silk pajamas. With one hand he scratched the long chestnut hair that stood up in disturbed clumps above his forehead, and with the other he scratched his crotch. She saw the blunt head of his penis poking out through the pajama fly and looked away in embarrassment. The sleep lines around his large blood shot brown eyes had not yet had a chance to straighten themselves out. He frowned and squinted at her, baring strong white teeth.

"Who are you?" he grumbled sleepily, digging his knuckles into his eyes and yawning fiercely. His broad Slavic face was cat-like.

"It's after twelve o'clock. Noon. Remember now?"

"No. I wake up at noon everyday," he said sourly, scratching his crotch again. She wished he wouldn't do that, because once again he exposed himself to her.

"Jennifer Sorel," she said.

"Ding dong," he rumbled thickly. "Ding ding. The bells ring. Give me a minute, I'll remember...."

He looked her up and down, obviously pleased by what he saw. He lifted his eyebrows when he studied her breasts, and he was awake—she could see it in his eyes, as obvious as sunrise.

"You're beautiful. Breath-taking. Of course, I remember *now*. The photographer. Snap snap, click click. Come on in. Let me help you carry these things. But first, first...."

With a grand, sweeping bow, he kissed her fingers. "My God, how could I have forgotten?" he asked, shaking his head. He picked up two of her bags and led the way down a long corridor lined with expensively framed ballet posters announcing his engagements around the world. Jennifer followed him in a daze, feeling such a helpless victim of infatua-

## Book Five

tion that in sheer self-defense she stopped, put the lights she was carrying down, and reached for her Nikon. Fiddling it into focus, she took a picture of Yuri putting her bags down in the middle of the room.

He heard the click and whirled. "WHAT ARE YOU DOING?" he shouted angrily in his thick Russian accent.

She was so intimidated she stuttered: "I-I thought . . . perhaps a candid shot. Just warming up," she added lamely.

"NO CANDID SHOTS! *Nyet!* Nix!"

Jennifer remained collected, despite her confusion. She was used to dealing with temperamental stars, but this was behavior she hadn't experienced before.

"Don't scream at me," she said quietly but firmly. "I'm sorry if I startled you."

He shook his head as if to clear it. His thick eyebrows lifted like wings. His fleshy nose twitched. Then he grinned.

"I apologize, Miss Sorel. In my country, cameras are weapons. Candid shots are taken by the secret police. I reacted without thinking."

"I'm here to take pictures for your book about how you escaped Russia. I'm Jennifer Sorel."

"You said that."

"You seem to need to be reminded."

He let out his breath in a *whoosh* of air and relaxed.

"You are a strong woman."

"I am what I have to be. I like who I am."

"You like taking pictures of Russian louts who wake up from gaudy Czarist dreams and behave boorishly toward you?"

"You *are* Yuri Muscovy," she reminded him, as she had reminded herself.

"You mean you're ready to put up with my bad temper?" His lower lip dropped and he flung himself on the rumpled brass bed beneath the chandelier. Stretched out on the bed he crossed his ankles and looked impudently at her.

*As if*, she thought, *Dostoyevsky had created Mick Jagger*.

She looked warily at him. He was smiling at her, stretched out flat on the sheets. No, it wasn't a smile, she decided; not a smile at all. It was a lustful smirk.

"You're not ready to shoot. Maybe I should come back after you've had something to eat."

He sprang up from the bed and began to pace the room in his pajamas. Jennifer stared boldly at the round smooth bulge of his buttocks and the smaller bulge of his genitals in front. She couldn't help but remember Alain. It had been too long. . . .

"I don't know what to do with women like you. I admit that. They come to me, my American fans, and I don't know what to do. I think sometimes that my dance is meaningless to them. That they want more than any man can offer. The *entrechat* for them does not dazzle; it is merely an introduction. Please, can you explain what American women want?"

"I can't, Mr. Muscovy."

"Yuri. I am Yuri with a woman of such surpassing beauty."

"Don't ask me to explain American women, Yuri. It would take too much time away from us."

"But you could." She nodded and flashed her teeth.

It was obvious that she could, and quite effectively—which he acknowledged with an impish grimace.

He struck a pose, spreading his arms wide and flashing his teeth. She aimed the Nikon in his direction half-heartedly, and politely clicked off a dozen shots.

"This is not what I want," she told him at last.

"What do you want?"

"Some reality," she answered firmly. "Not the same old poses."

"I'm hung-over. I'm tired, and you want me to be inventive."

He needed some stroking, that's what it was, she decided. She put her arms around him and pressed her body to his, mashing her full breasts against his pajama front. His arms circled her narrow waist and pulled her still closer.

"You feel wonderful," he said. "Your heart is like a rabbit in your chest. You wear clothing that excites a man who dances with creatures without sex."

He pulled her skirt up from behind and touched her naked buttocks, cupping them and pressing her against his erection. His wide mouth crushed hers and his tongue slipped between her teeth. "I want you now," he grunted. "Right here on the rug." He was demanding and strong and she felt herself surrendering to her years of unrequited ardor. But her clothes—

"Wait," she breathed apologetically. "Let me get out of my suit."

"Clothes?" he cried, hooking his hand in the neck of her white silk suit and ripping it downwards, exposing her nipples to the air. He pushed his pajama bottoms off and stepped away from them, brandishing a magnificent erection at her, cupping his fat balls in both hands and moving toward her as if bringing a gift.

He swept her up in his arms and carried her across the room to the rumpled four poster bed where she lay flat on her back in garter belt and stockings, her breasts heaving, waiting for the great dancer to make a grand leap and impale her on his aroused penis. Everything was happening as she had daydreamed it. Overwhelming, romantic passion, and the thrill of knowing that he wanted her so badly he would ravish her. If she'd resisted, he would have forced her.

The hungry look in his eyes as he stared down at the riches of her golden body excited her. She parted her legs and let him see how wet she was for him.

"Take me, Yuri. It's all for you."

She closed her eyes and waited for his muscular body to fall on her, anticipating the weight upon her, his warmth, the odor of his arousal.

She was shocked at his stinging words and her eyes popped open.

"You're a slut. A temptress. . . ."

At first she didn't understand. Perhaps it was his accent. What was he talking about? He had her pinned naked to the bed, within ten minutes of meeting him, and he seemed to be cursing her. She reached for him but he jerked away from her. She was shocked when he stood up and began to pace the Persian rug before the bed wearing only his pajama tops.

"No!" he exclaimed passionately, running his fingers through his hair as if a demon had sunk its talons in his scalp.

"What is it, Yuri? Come make love to me, please." She called to him but it was as if he didn't hear.

He stood at the foot of the bed and glared at her. She looked at his strong dancer's thighs and the heavy flesh of his genitals when he spoke. His voice was thick with emotion and his penis was semi-erect.

"No! I save everything, every ounce of energy, for dance. I am sorry I gave you the wrong impression of me."

"Yuri, don't be crazy."

What the hell was going on? Jennifer searched his eyes: she saw lust, fear, longing and indecision in them—and depths she could not interpret.

She sighed regretfully and sat up on the bed.

"I wish I liked to smoke cigarettes," she told him. "I think now would be the time for one."

"I will dress properly, and then perhaps we can behave toward each other in a more civilized manner. I will pose for you. You will get pictures that will be reprinted forever in histories of the dance."

"I don't understand. You all but knocked me off my feet. . . ."

"I am not to be questioned, Miss Sorel," he said coldly, striding across the big room to an ornate oak wardrobe. He flung open the door and took out a white cotton peasant blouse and a pair of pressed Levis. As he dressed he talked, and a thick lock of chestnut hair fell over his white forehead.

"I am ashamed of the way I greeted you. It's not my nature to attack perfect strangers. America is so seductive that I think I must have everything I see immediately. I become like a small child because everything seems so available. . . . Like fruit on trees, the ripe bodies of American women. I'm sorry. . . ."

Jennifer sat up in bed, pulling the sheets over her breasts. Her eyes blazed.

"Don't be sorry about attacking me. Just be sorry that you didn't finish what you started. You were fulfilling a particular fantasy of mine that I've nourished for half a dozen years. What you don't realize is that American women—at least *this* American woman— make their own choices. When you touched me it was with my eager approval. Don't you realize the power you have over women, Yuri?"

It was apparent that what she said surprised him.

"Thank you for saying that to me. Your dignity is adequate reproof for my crudity." He spoke stiffly to her.

"You're not understanding me, Yuri. I don't think you were crude, and as far as I'm concerned you have nothing to apologize to me for except that you didn't carry through. I mean, you shouldn't start something you don't want to finish."

He sucked in air. "Is this true?" he said with amazement. "Surely you are saying this just to make me feel better that I was an animal."

She jumped from the bed and put her arms around his neck. Her hands caressed his thick chestnut locks, and she held his eyes with her own. What she had to say was important to her.

"Look, Yuri. I'm a photographer. I take pictures of people. Some I like, some I don't like. You I've always been infatuated with. When I see you dance, I feel myself in your body—and I want to make love to you."

He was reassured enough to put his arms around her and pull her to his broad chest.

"I don't know how to make this up to you. I think perhaps the best thing I can do is to pose for you in ways I have never shown other photographers."

"All I want is that you act as you would normally."

"Don't be silly," he told her, putting one long finger to her lips to quiet her. "I'll give you what I've never given another photographer."

Duty called. Jennifer looked around for her clothes and saw them in shreds on the floor near the bed.

"But what am I to wear?" she asked disconsolately.

"Are you cold?" he asked solicitously.

"I'm naked and you're dressed. Yes, I need clothes."

"Well," he said, scratching his square jaw thoughtfully. He looked around, and then snapped his fingers. He strode to his wardrobe and threw it open. He stood before a rack of clothing for a moment and then pulled out an ermine coat which he threw casually to her.

She caught it the way a child catches a star. She snuggled into it.

"It fits you perfectly. The woman I bought it for ran off with my brother. I take great pleasure in offering it to you."

"It's so warm!"

The smile split his craggy Russian face. His eyes glowed with the happiness of offering her a present.

"Now you must take pretty pictures of me. I won't stand in the way of your career any longer."

Jennifer swallowed the words in her throat. They would be confusing; they didn't need to be said. She started unpacking her equipment and setting up lights. The activity helped soothe her.

"What should I do?" he offered when he saw her struggling under the weight of her equipment.

"Go shave. I like your beard, but I think most people would rather see a smooth cheek on their ballet star."

He blushed like a little boy and nodded. He walked to the bathroom and closed the door behind him.

*Whew!* Jennifer took a deep breath. She was glad to have a brief respite from the whirling Dervish known as Yuri Muscovy. It gave her time to set up her lights. She placed her Nikon on a tripod and busied herself with the time-consuming details of preparing for a shooting.

When Yuri came out of the bathroom he looked composed and calm. The sight of Jennifer's camera and her lights seemed to have a salutary effect on him. He smiled reflexively and she frowned, hoping that he wasn't going to go into one of the familiar routines that celebrities practiced before a mirror and presented to every photographer.

"What do you want me to do?" he asked. "Pretend to be other people," she told him. "Other dancers."

He liked the idea. Pretending offered him new territory.

He lifted his arms above his head and began to dance.

"This is a simple folk dance," he explained to her as his feet beat a tattoo on the polished wide board floor. "This is Rudi Nureyev, for instance." Jennifer watched with growing astonishment as he impersonated Nureyev's dance style so exactly that she had to laugh for the sheer magic involved.

"You've studied him," she giggled, snapping the shutter of her camera click-click-click.

"Rudi and I are friends. He is such a master he is easy to imitate."

"Please take off your clothes and do more."

"People will be shocked."

"People will see the absolute beauty of your body."

She had appealed to his vanity.

"Yes, I suppose that is true."

He took off his clothes and danced for her, quite plausibly doing perfect reflections of the movements of Baryshnikov and Peter Martins. He made a stage of the plush hotel room.

At last she called "enough." When Yuri stopped there was only the faintest sheen of sweat on his handsome Russian face. He was in such perfect condition, despite his hangover, that his body seemed tireless, almost an inhuman machine, a thing of pulleys and weights.

"Do you have your requirement of pictures? I have tried to compensate for my bad behavior of earlier."

She touched his cheek. "I know you have, and I should be happy."

"But . . . ? Why are you not happy?"

"These shots are not very exciting, Yuri. I wanted you to explode for me—to be very loose."

He broke in the middle of a movement and looked at her, stiff as a Kabuki figure. "I *am* a dancer. I am *loose!*"

"No. You're caught in what you do. I want a picture of you, not you in a role, or an impersonation. *You*. Can you understand that?"

"Yes," he said hesitantly, touching her breasts as if for reassurance. She let herself move into his hands, but he pulled away. "What would you like me to do?" he asked her.

"Come outside. Maybe on the street I will see a photograph that will prove to be true."

"True?"

"You know, authentic. Let me explain: I'm looking for a photograph of you that takes you away from dance as a formal structure, which is where you hide. I'm looking for what I call 'the hit.'"

"What is it?"

"I know it when I see it. It's when what I see in my mind matches up with what I catch through the lens. Snap at that exact moment, and I've got what I came for."

Yuri paced back and forth. His face was red and he looked restless. Agitated.

"Are you all right?" she asked.

"Yes, yes. But let's take a walk. I want some fresh

air. Maybe outside you'll see the picture you're looking for."

"You'd better put something on, don't you think?"

"I'll wear my down coat. We'll both be naked underneath."

They would be very fashionable, Jennifer thought, remembering Nikki's nakedness under her full-length beaver.

They were alone in the corridor outside of his suite. He took her arm and Jennifer became a fan again, fantasizing that they were lovers on the way to one of his performances at Lincoln Center.

The elevator doors opened with a soft *ping* and they stepped inside. Yuri wore soft boots and the long down coat reached to his ankles. They stood facing each other in silence—and then Yuri's eyes flashed and he reached out for her.

Pulling open her coat he filled his fingers with her breasts, handling them roughly before moving his hands to between her legs. His penis stood up like an iron bar between them, and he pulled one of her legs up to his waist so he could insert himself into her. He thrust with powerful, rapid strokes and her body shuddered under the impact of his buffeting. Her fingernails ripped the skin of his back and she grunted in a kind of sexual delirium. He was piercing her all the way to the bottom of her lust.

*Ding*, the elevator announced their eminent arrival on the lobby floor.

He whispered into her ear: "We have ten seconds and I'm going to shoot my sperm up inside you, you beautiful luscious piece of ass, you wonderful fucking American pussy. . . ."

*Ding* again. "Ohhhh," he groaned, driving into her. Her body vibrated from her knees to her shoulders with the power of his orgasm.

"Oh give it all to me, Yuri," she breathed.

He stepped away from her, his penis only slightly less stiff than it had been a minute before, a drop of semen at its tip. They just had time to close their long coats before the steel doors slid open and they stepped out into the lobby of the Hotel St. Etienne.

Their faces were red and they were still gasping for breath when two of Yuri's fans recognized him. He frowned petulantly—like a child who's been having fun who is called to kiss his parents goodnight—but he accepted their ballpoint pens and signed his name to the shopping bags they carried. The two matronly women looked enviously in Jennifer's direction and Yuri shot her a wolfish grin.

She knew by the expression on his face that she was going to be able to get the picture she wanted. He licked his lips as if he could eat her up.

"Let's go back upstairs, Jennifer."

# II

JENNIFER was running down a beach in Tobago and she tripped. The sand rushed up at her face—and she awoke to find herself flat on her back in Yuri Muscovy's bedroom in his Hotel St. Etienne suite. Yuri lay sprawled across her naked body snoring like a drunken Russian peasant. After one of those erotic matinee dreams that seem more vivid for being uncompleted, she awoke in a darkened hotel room feeling buried.

She tried to suggest with the gentlest of pushes that Yuri should roll over, but he was out cold, an-

## Book Five

chored to her by the large hand that cupped her between the legs.

She kissed his temple and blew in his ear, but he was a stone. She squirmed to the right, squirmed to the left, and at last managed to ease herself from under his weight. She had never imagined that a ballet dancer, those winged beings, could be so *heavy*.

She slid off the side of the bed and he caught her ankle, making her fall back.

She felt something wet and warm on her toes and realized that he had taken them in his mouth, which made her shiver.

"*You women in a hurry!*" he growled. "Come back here."

"Yuri, I have to pee."

"Oh?" His hand played with her breasts, pinching the nipples.

"I'll be right back."

He relaxed his fingers and she slipped free, stumbling across the thick hotel rug with a pounding head. In her infatuated foolishness she had tried to match Yuri drink for drink when they returned to his room. While they made love, he paused occasionally to drink. When they rested, he drank. Stolichnaya on ice. He'd held the bottle of vodka up to her, brandished it in her face, saying "This is my Russian blood and sperm." When she made a face and told him that in her experience men who had too much to drink couldn't take full advantage of a sexual encounter, he had roared out his reply.

"That's an American problem! When *I* drink I fuck hard and sure—like a god—and the more I drink the more I fuck."

Jennifer knew better, but her initial skepticism had been replaced by a kind of dumbstruck wonder by the time Yuri dozed off atop her after his fourth volcanic eruption.

She went directly to the window where she peeked through the heavy velvet drapes out at bustling Fifth Avenue and reassured herself that after all that had happened, it was still afternoon in the Real World. She had been lost to it for several hours while she danced, horizontally, opposite the great Muscovy. She took a deep breath and threw back her shoulders, letting the heavy drapes fall closed on the outside world again.

The bathroom was white and cavernous and old-fashioned, dominated by a huge bathtub that looked big enough to hide several generations of Rockefellers, if revolution ever came to Fifth Avenue. It had a curved bottom and sat on claw feet on the white tile floor.

There were floor-to-ceiling mirrors around the room, a few large potted plants, and a bidet next to the toilet. A vase of daisies sat atop a chest where Jennifer found thick bath towels.

She would take a luxurious bath while Yuri slept off the vodka, and then perhaps she could persuade him to make love to her again. The thought made her tingle.

While the water slowly filled the great tub she stood before one of the mirrors inspecting herself. Her motive was less personal vanity than a respect for nature's bounty. If she found flaws she strove assiduously to correct them with exercise and diet. Flab and sag were against her principles.

Her tan was fading, she noted ruefully, but her golden skin glowed with good health. She was five feet seven inches of immaculately assembled American woman, blessed with mythic good looks: small arched feet with toenails painted mauve; firm round calves curving into slender thighs; clipped tawny maidenhair covering a soft swollen pubis; a flat belly, high firm breasts and swollen pink nipples.

She turned and looked over her shoulder at the attributes her admirers gazed so fondly upon whenever she walked away from them. The cheeks of her ass were firm round globes that quivered if she tensed her legs and bounced slightly. Her back was a slender tree growing from the fullness of her hips and the smallness of her waist. Her shoulder blades were delicate beginnings of wings.

The results of her impromptu inventory were satisfactory. The life force at the center of her being had been granted a splendid palace of flesh in which to work out its destiny.

She imagined Alain watching her and felt a burning sensation between her legs. She couldn't get him out of her mind. Yuri was a fantasy, plain and simple, but Alain!

After relieving herself, she settled herself on the bidet next to the toilet. She always felt hedonistic turning on the jets of water to cleanse herself—which in turn brought on more agreeable sensations. She felt Yuri's semen being washed from her.

*Ooooooooohhhhhh,* she crooned to herself. *The French knew what they were doing when they invented this water toy.* When she turned off the water she felt marvelous. Rosy inside.

She was dancing before the mirrors with her arms up and she noticed a new growth of light curly hair in her armpits. Checking the tub, she figured she had plenty of time to shave them; she looked through Yuri's medicine chest for a razor.

The blade of the safety razor slid through the shaving soap under Jennifer's arm with such slick efficiency that she had to be careful she didn't get carried away. Shaving was sexy because it resulted in smoothness of skin, and smooth skin was sensuous —on it your fingers could slide anywhere. . . .

When he walked into the bathroom rubbing his

eyes Yuri found Jennifer shaving the edges of her pubic triangle, one foot propped on the bidet. She didn't look up until she finished.

"What are you doing? I don't like bald women!"

"I was waiting for the bath water to run and I was killing time. Result? Discovery. Shaving is a very sexy thing to do. Did you know that?"

She looked pointedly at his chest, which was covered with tight, curly dark hair. He looked down at it, and back to her.

"Oh no you don't," he said. He grabbed her, pulling her against him bearishly, her cheek over his heart.

She pulled at the tightly coiled hair on his chest until he made a face. "Let me shave *you*, Yuri. Please? Trust me?"

"Oh, you hot bitch. I can't refuse you. . . . Go on, if it will tickle your fancy."

"Something like that," she grinned. He waited like a martyr bravely expecting the worst, and then his resolve faded and he insisted that he needed a drink and she had to allow him to find the bottle of vodka.

He returned with a straight-backed chair and the vodka. "My anesthetic," he grinned happily, patting the bottle and seating himself before one of the large gilt edged mirrors. She marveled at his posture: he sat perfectly erect despite the copious amount of alcohol in his bloodstream. His thick lips twisted with amusement as he watched Jennifer apply hot towels and then shaving cream to his chest. He was an indulgent lord, brave enough to hold still while a woman brandished a razor up and down his chest.

"This is very funny," he chuckled into the mirror.

"Don't laugh too hard, Narcissus. My hand might

slip and you'll end up looking like the girl of your dreams."

He growled affectionately at her—following her hand when she pulled the safety razor down his snowy chest with eyes that kept darting back to her breasts.

The cold steel slid smoothly over his skin, between his nipples and over his broad rib cage. Jennifer worked with steady long strokes, mesmerized by her task.

Yuri was entranced with what he saw in the mirror in back of Jennifer. She was kneeling on the tile and her plump round ass wiggled as she worked. Lower he saw the small dark triangle of her sex winking suggestively at him.

He took another drink. By now his chest was bare as a baby's bottom. Jennifer stood up and beamed approvingly at her work. Now his chest could be kissed. She knelt before him and kissed his right nipple, which was copper-colored and swollen. Her soft lips nibbled awhile before sucking it erect. Her tongue brushed it, her teeth nipped it. Then she moved across his chest to pay homage to his left nipple.

Yuri rolled his brown eyes back in his head and groaned aloud. His penis jutted stiffly upward.

*"Never before,"* he moaned with such sincerity that she almost believed him. From what she'd heard Russian women were plodders in bed, but on the other hand he'd been in America for too long not to have experienced such exotic delights with the multitudes of dance groupies available to a star.

She explored every inch of his newly smooth chest with her lips and fingernails before she bowed her head in obeisance and took the round head of his penis in her warm mouth. She felt the heat rising in her blood just as the first water from the overflowing bath washed over her feet.

"The bath!" she cried, springing up and running to it. She plunged her hands into the warm water and turned the faucets off. Hot water splashed over the side of the huge tub onto her thighs—and felt wonderful.

Yuri was close behind her, his hands on her buttocks, his right index finger exploring the warm wetness between her legs. Jennifer let some of the water out, then replaced the stopper.

"Let's take a bath together!"

"Will you fuck me underwater?"

"I'll take you on the cold tiles if you don't climb in."

They sank together in the warmth. The water was up around their necks and their arms and legs floated almost weightlessly. Jennifer found that she couldn't keep her legs together; they floated up and apart, offering Yuri an irresistible target. The water distorted the angles of their bodies.

He pushed himself under her and maneuvered his semi-stiff penis between her thighs, but the buoyancy of the water made their connection as difficult as refueling a rocket in outer space. When he accomplished it she thrashed her legs in the water and put her arms around him so they wouldn't float apart. He began to make love to her with the deliberate movements of slow motion photography—and then abruptly he rose to his feet with her still impaled upon him, stunning her with the strength required by such a move. Dripping water like Poseidon rising from the waves, he rode her to furious climax, their impassioned cries echoing off the tile walls.

# 12

It was the last day of the old year and three quarters of the nation was blanketed in white. After hovering around zero for weeks, the mercury plummeted to some disagreeable new low like minus 23 in the northeastern states and remained stuck there, frozen perhaps, by the wind chill factor.

The state of Vermont was colder than a walk-in freezer, and the narrow road that winds up steep hill and down deep dale through the Green Mountain National Forest was snow banked higher on both sides than the roof of Marina Sorel's beloved and battered yellow 1968 Porsche.

She and Jennifer had driven from Manhattan to attend a New Year's weekend celebration at the country home of Jack August, who—in addition to the other more mysterious roles Jennifer had seen him play—was her editor and inspiration, as well as the publisher of *New Man* magazine.

The road was dark and daunting and large, wet, white crystals of snow were driven in windblown waves against the windshield, each of them illumined for a moment by the headlights, where they sparkled like a shower of diamonds.

It was warm and cozy inside the car. Marina drove with fearless aplomb while holding up her end of a non-stop conversation. There was the sense of covering ground.

For hours as the pearly afternoon light waned the twins had exchanged news. Jennifer had told her stories about Alain and Nikki Armitage and John Hamilton and even her bathtub scene with Yuri Muscovy, and Marina had responded with the latest head count of eligible bachelors and an episodic recital of her love affair with their host, Jack August. As they got closer to their destination in the mountains somewhere outside Brattleboro, the sisters felt pressed to talk from the deepest recesses of their overburdened hearts.

"Jack August will not surrender one iota of his precious independence," Marina complained.

"But why should he?" Jennifer asked. "Why should anyone?"

"I don't know, Jennifer. Sometimes you're so idealistic I am left breathless. Speechless."

"Well, I'm entranced by Nikki and Alain exactly because they haven't lost one bit of independence. They do what they like when they feel like doing it."

"That's easy. All it takes is enough money . . .

## Book Five

You know the illusions great money mothers. No, I don't like being so impulsive. . . ."

"I think I've enjoyed being impulsive more than you have trying to keep up with Jack."

Marina nodded in the darkness.

"You know what he said to me when I offered in utter innocence to help him out with this pajama party we're driving to? He said he'd rather have his secretary make the arrangements just in case he decided he didn't want to talk with me before this weekend. I mean—the bastard!"

The pain in Marina's voice reminded Jennifer of her own unresolved feelings about Jack August. For one exciting month she had shared his affections with her beautiful twin sister, before deciding that the sanest course was flight.

"I guess what bothered me most about the three of us together was that Jack was more interested in power than he was in us. Or love. Or sex."

"Look, Sis, we're almost there. Tell me about you. I don't want to talk about Jack anymore."

"Facts? I think I'm in love with Alain. But his sister Nikki won't let him go. That's it, that's the whole story."

"A seductive combination—and crazy. Why not just let them go? But then, I guess I said that before."

"Why don't you let go of Jack?"

"That bad, huh?"

"There's something about Alain that keeps me intrigued."

"And Yuri?"

"He's crazier than they are!"

"But Yuri Muscovy, he's a god! I wouldn't let such a man walk away from me."

"Well, I'll introduce him to you if you like."

"No. I've got my hands full with Jack."

Jennifer thought it was time to change the subject. "It looks so cold out there—*brrr*. I hope they have a *giant* fire going."

They turned off the storybook main road onto an even curvier side road. After that, Marina drove slowly, crossing two stone bridges and then turning left after clattering over a wooden covered bridge, spinning the wheels of the faithful Porsche up a steeply mounting road that turned on itself and then leveled out. It brought them at last to the only house on the road, a rambling stone structure, with large outbuildings behind it, that had been built in the 1920s in imitation of the Georgian style.

There were other cars in the driveway—a Mercedes and a Volvo, and the outside spotlights were on to show them where they could park. A large black dog romped out of the house to greet them.

Jennifer patted the big retriever on its massive head and looked up at a night sky which was throwing light puffs of cold cotton down on them. The spotlights outlined each crystalline flake. They had arrived at an ice palace at the end of the world.

Jack August came out of the house to help with the suitcases they were pulling out of the Porsche. He grabbed two of the heaviest bags and trudged off through the snow to the house, calling over his shoulder.

"Hi, Marina! Hi, Jenny! Welcome to the North Pole! Watch your step, it's a little slippery here."

Hearing his strong voice brought everything back, and Jennifer's knees got so weak for a moment that she slipped and might have fallen if Marina hadn't caught her arm.

"Watch it, Sis."

"I thought I was cured. I was sure."

In the foyer he took their furs and held them away from him disapprovingly, as if they'd brought

## Book Five

him a fresh kill; he thought it was barbaric that beautiful, fashionable women would wear the skins of wild animals.

He hadn't lost one iota of attractiveness that Jennifer could see. Coal black hair still rose in a widow's peak above his high forehead, his large nose was still imperious (the small bump in it only made him look more like a leader, a warrior, a conqueror) and his lips were still carved and sensual. His brown eyes could change quickly from amusement to contempt. He was a man of power, and the high collar of the white wool turtleneck sweater he wore under a tweed jacket made Jennifer think of a ruff around a king's neck.

He put his arms around both of them and led them into the living room, where he kissed Jennifer with soft, slightly parted lips, murmuring, "You smell as good as ever."

When he released her she sagged inside. His charm was his ability to focus totally on a woman, even for just a minute—to make a lasting impression on her with one or two small attentions.

The room was comfortable, cozy, and rustic. Painted screens, antique chairs, silk shaded lamps, oak flooring, and in the middle of it all a hooked rug before the fire on which lounged the black retriever who had greeted them.

Sitting in a rocking chair before the fire was a guest who had arrived before them. Her lush figure strained the fabric of the red jump suit she wore. Her eyelids were painted blue, and she wore her coppery hair in a page boy. When she stood up to greet the twins a pair of glasses fell from her lap. She was slightly and endearingly nearsighted.

"This is Misty. She's involved in a project I'm working on. A very nice lady—and you'd better not forget it or she'll remind you."

"Hi, Misty," Jennifer said, offering her hand. Marina looked sulky and only nodded.

"Hi. You must be cold. Come on, get closer to the fire. There's enough for all of us."

There was real solicitousness in the woman's tone. Jennifer stepped closer to the fire, grateful for its heat.

"You know what? Just like Jack promised, you look so good I have to tell you that you do. You understand that, don't you?" The voice was husky, low, thoughtful.

Jennifer thought that maybe she was in the presence of a distinctly foreign mode of thought, and she was fascinated.

"I understand. How do you know Jack?" She angled her body so that her feet were warmed by the fire. She wanted to know about Misty, and she wanted to keep her toes toasty.

"Boy, that's a question I don't know if I can answer. Jack invested in a movie I made, okay? And he came around a lot to watch. It was, I have to admit, a sex film—fortunately for all of us, including of course Mr. Jack August—it made a lot of money. "Birds Of Paradise." You probably saw the ads."

"I didn't know that Jack invested in movies."

"Between you and me, I think he was just playing around."

Jennifer leaned her head closer to Misty. She was enjoying their conversation. She saw Jack leaning on a corner of the mantel talking while Marina warmed her backside as she listened, her jaw jutted upward attentively.

"What do you do, Jenny?" Misty asked her.

"I'm a photographer."

"What kind of pictures do you take?"

"Oh, anything. Actually, I'm always at a loss

about how to answer that question. I just finished taking some pictures of Yuri Muscovy."

"I don't know who he is. Do you ever take pictures of women and men doing things? I mean, X-rated things."

"I've done a couple of centerfolds that were pretty sexy. . . ."

"Do you get hot? I mean, while you're taking the pictures?"

Jennifer nodded. "Sometimes."

Misty clapped her hands like a delighted five-year-old.

"I'm so glad you didn't say"—and here she pinched an upturned nose with her fingers—"'if you've seen one, you've seen 'em all,' like a lot of photographers do. I think if something turns you on, you should be able to talk about it. Don't you?"

"I couldn't agree more," Jennifer said. She could see that they were going to be friends; she was intrigued by Misty's innocent earthiness.

She heard the pop of a champagne cork and Marina announced that it was time to make a farewell toast to the old year.

"It was a pretty good one for me," Misty said. Jack brought glasses of Dom Perignon for everyone, and they stood around the fire sipping, listening to Guy Lombardo music on the local Vermont station and thinking about 1981.

Jack brought Jennifer more champagne and complimented her on the brown wool dress she was wearing.

"It's country chic if I ever saw it, but the nicest thing about it is how it clings to you."

Jennifer winked good-naturedly at him, more sisterly than sultry.

"Forecast for me, Jack. What about 1982?"

"I'm going to give you a serious answer, Jenny. Business. In six weeks your spread on male sexuality in *New Man* pulled a whole lot of mail. Look after your career. Let's talk about what you should do next for *New Man*."

"There was something I wanted to talk to you about."

Before she could say anything more her twin sister interrupted them by putting her arms around Jack's neck and pulling his face down for a passionate kiss, which he made even more passionate running his hands up and down her body. Jennifer and Misty kissed on the cheek and smiled, left out.

Somewhere a clock struck twelve times.

# 13

They spent the day skiing on nearby Mount Snow, and came back to Jack's house thoroughly chilled. Marina made hot toddies and Jack went off to prepare his hot tub for them.

Jennifer stood shivering before the newly prepared fire, where she was joined by her twin. Misty sat in the rocking chair pulling off her boots. She was feeling sore because she'd fallen a few times on the beginner's slope. Had Jack invited her for this weekend on a whim? Was she meant to serve as his foil, someone to keep the Sorel twins from joining forces?

"Oh, I'm stiff," she groaned, dropping her boots on the floor.

"I think we all are," Marina said. "This is my first time on the slopes this year."

"Have you ever been rubbed with oil?" Misty asked.

"Not in a long time."

"I'll rub you both down before we climb into the hot tub. You'll feel like you died and went to heaven, and I'll work the kinks out of my shoulders."

"How wonderful. Where did you learn massage?"

Jennifer's single question started Misty talking about herself, in a form of free association that her listeners found fascinating.

"I learned massage in a massage parlor. Not that you ever give a real massage in one of those places, but I went to school and studied it. That's how I got into my own business, with my own stable of girls."

"But how did you meet Jack?" Marina wanted all the particulars.

"He backed a film I was in. I don't know why. . . ."

In the room where the hot tub had been set up there was a massage table. Jennifer and Marina stepped quickly out of their clothes.

Jennifer stretched out on the table and rested her cheek on her wrists. She was going to enjoy this. Misty's hands spread thick oil over her shoulder blades and back, and dug hard fingers into the knots she encountered there. Jennifer moaned gratefully as she felt relaxation spread through her winter-tightened body in gentle waves.

"You have magical hands," she told Misty. "I'm melting."

"Your body is so beautiful! You know you two could make a fortune in my line?"

"People have told us that before," Jennifer said. She winked at her twin, who lay prone on the next table waiting her turn. Marina's tan was perfect, despite the season. The half moons of her ass quivered deliciously when she moved. Her long black hair fell over her naked back like a fan. Jennifer wondered if people would think her narcissistic if she told them that Marina's body was the most perfect she'd ever seen.

"Oh, sweet glory, this hot tub is glorious," Misty said when she stepped out of her jump suit and climbed daintily into Jack's tub. Her breasts floated on the surface of the hot water, with large brown nipples that fascinated Jennifer because they seemed to be painted, they were so glossy.

Misty noticed her glance. "Aren't they great-looking painted? It's going to come off in the water, though. Oh well."

Jennifer lolled in the water, her head thrown back, her eyes closed. The hot water was so delicious, so warming. The massage and now the heat made her body feel better than it had since returning from the Tobago sun.

Jack sat in the water across from her, his hand resting casually on Misty's thigh. Marina sat on his other side with a tolerant smirk on her face. Jennifer hoped her sister wouldn't lose her temper.

"This is just the place to spend the first day of the new year," Jack sighed, reaching for a hot toddy. "And with the three most beautiful women I know."

"Do you think you can handle us all, Jack?" Marina asked. Uh-oh, Jennifer winced. She recognized the glint in her twin's eye—it was a danger sign.

Misty giggled. "Yeah. Maybe your eyes are bigger than your thing."

"We'll see," Jack answered complacently. "But I doubt it."

"This is most terrific I've felt since I got back from Tobago," Jennifer said.

"What were you doing down there?" Jack asked.

"I was taking pictures of Nikki Armitage. Do you remember her? Exotic, dark. . . ."

"Yes, I do. She dropped out of sight."

"I went down to the Caribbean with her and her brother, Alain."

"What kind of pictures did you get?"

"They are savage, Jack. Wait till you see them."

"Maybe they're for *New Man*."

"Tell Jack who Nikki and Alain Armitage are, Jenny," Marina prompted. "Tell him what you told me."

"Wait a minute," Jack said. "Aren't they related to that guru who's always getting headlines in those tabloids housewives read while they're standing in line at the supermarket?"

"Père Mitya is their father. They're half brother and sister."

"Père Mitya! That's the one, all right. Père Mitya and his sex cults. Orgasm as meditation. Good stuff."

"I've heard of him," Misty said. "Sounds kind of like a nut, but *my* kind of nut, if you know what I mean."

"I'd like to get some pictures of him and his group for *New Man*. Maybe we'll do a whole spread on the man."

"Should be easy to get."

"No, just the opposite. That's just it, Jen. He only sees one person at a time, ever, and his followers operate by themselves. No uniforms, or anything like that. They don't sell books in the bus station. There's only a few old photographs of Père Mitya around. None at all of his followers."

"I could talk to Alain and Nikki, if you wanted me to."

"Maybe they'll introduce you to him. It looks like it could be another cover story, if you want to do it."

Perhaps unconsciously, while he spoke Jack was playing with Misty's nipples. Jennifer wasn't sure, but she thought she could make out the porno star's hand in the water between Jack's thighs. Marina looked ready to blow her stack when at the last minute before eruption she had a more pleasant notion. She slid into the water on her knees until she was submerged below her shoulders.

Jack gazed down at her with the dispassionate regard of a man who weighs everything on his own scales. Marina's barely concealed jealousy seemed to spur him to greater provocations with Misty. By moving between his legs Marina was placing a claim on him.

"Misty," he asked the woman whose nipples he was pinching. "What would happen next in one of your films? I mean, three women and a man in a hot tub. What does the man do first?"

Marina rose in the water before him. "Stick your finger in me, Jack. That's what you should do first."

He pursed his lips and crinkled his eyes, and reached out with one finger to trace the outer lips of Marina's sex, dipping into the tight opening for more honey to spread over her vulva. His thumb pressed her clitoris.

Then his finger began to push into Marina's vagina with short slow strokes. His eyes were slitted with concentration as he manipulated her.

Jennifer felt a twinge in her belly, recalling Jack's fingers thrusting into her own body. She moved to get closer to them.

Marina was standing up, gyrating on Jack's middle finger; his palm cupped her between the legs as if he were holding her up. Misty had leaned forward and was licking the tip of Jack's thick penis.

His left hand was free, and with it he stroked Jennifer's breasts and belly, slipping his hand between her legs and curving his middle finger to hook into her palpitating opening.

"*Ohhh,*" she exhaled when she felt the first wonderful wave of sensation. She wanted it to be his cock in her, but his finger was hard and forceful as it stabbed in and out. Like Marina beside her, she gyrated on the fulcrum of his finger, rolling her hips and thrashing in the water.

It was as if he held them in the palms of his hands and could bounce them up and down, could make them dance like puppets. Jennifer leaned forward and seized his nipple with her teeth, gently tugging at it, tongue licking the soft flesh. Jack groaned and closed his eyes.

"I want to put it in you, Jenny," he told her, removing his finger and pulling her to his lap. Misty helped position her on his legs in the water so that she was facing away from him and his penis was deep inside her. In this position her breasts were available to his hands, and she could feel his mouth on her neck, his teeth nibbling at her skin.

"Ride him, Jenny," Marina encouraged her.

She bounced faster and faster in his lap, feeling the ridges and veins of his iron-hard penis rub against a place so deep inside her she didn't think it had ever been touched before. The wonderful fire was playing all over her body, leaping from nerve to nerve, and any moment Jack was going to explode inside her and for that moment would belong to her —and her alone.

But he slipped out of her, he was thrusting so

vigorously, and she cried in frustration: "Oh, put it back, I have to have it back inside me! Please oh please don't take it away."

In vain. Marina and Misty had become allies, and swooped on Jack, making waves in the warm water. Misty seized his erection and helped guide Marina as she sank down on it with a hissing sigh of satisfaction.

"Oh, thank God. You saved it for me. I want you to shoot off while I ride you."

"I'm getting close," he warned her. "It's bubbling up in me like hot oil."

Marina tossed her head back and forth in a frenzy, flipping her black hair in front of her face. Misty stroked her breasts and Jennifer, so close to her own edge, rubbed herself frantically, watching for an opening with Jack.

She knelt in the water beside Misty and cupped Jack's balls as they swung smoothly through the water. She squeezed them and made a circle of her fingers to fasten around the base of his cock when it emerged from her sister's cunt.

They were building a pyramid of desire and he was the base; the three women anticipated his every whim, interpreting his needs before he had to open his mouth. They moved together in the hot tub like a new form of aquatic life.

They all sensed when it was time, when he could no longer contain the pressures building up in his system. His eyes widened as if he saw something they didn't, and his fingers clawed between Jennifer and Misty's legs, plugging them into a four way connection with himself and Marina, his entire body shaking with the effort to share his climax with the three women, his arms and wrists moving like pistons as he rocked his hips under Marina.

*"This is it!"* he cried when it happened at last. "Come with me—all of us at the same time!"

It was an especially auspicious way to begin the new year.

## 14

A LIGHT snow fell. It was that time of the evening when the street lamps have switched on but it is not yet dark outside. Jennifer walked quickly down East Sixty-fifth Street and stopped before a familiar building, one of the more attractive brownstones on the street. It was here that Nikki had brought her, blindfolded, to meet Alain.

On the phone John Hamilton had told her that Nikki and Alain were in Europe. She had not been able to conceal her disappointment very well.

"Oh," she said with a distressed sigh.

"Can I help?"

111

She told him briefly about her desire to photograph Père Mitya and his followers.

"Why is *New Man* interested? This 'sex cult' business again, I suppose." His courteous voice turned scornful.

"John, you know me. I'm not going to do any harm with my camera."

"Come this evening at six. We'll talk."

She mounted the eight stone steps to the ornately carved door feeling excited but apprehensive about seeing John Hamilton again. He was an attractive, powerful figure who had kept his distance while they were on Tobago. An intriguing challenge.

The door opened before she had a chance to press the doorbell and she was so surprised she took a step backward.

It was Shairoon, the woman who had danced every evening on the beach until she had succeeded in seducing the haughty John Hamilton.

"Come in," she said, lowering her eyes and holding the heavy door open.

"It's so nice to see you again, Shairoon. This is really a surprise!"

Shairoon beamed and held out her hands for Jennifer's ermine coat, which sparkled with snow.

Jennifer picked at her hair in the full length mirror and decided that she had chosen the right look, simple, elegant, understated—a green silk wrap, a black velvet choker.

"Mister John Hamilton wants to see you in the trophy room. It's this way."

She followed Shairoon up the curving staircase, admiring the way the native dancer seemed to float as she ascended.

Jennifer expected that a trophy room would contain large metal cups and placques, the usual testimonials to success and athletic prowess, but the Armitage trophy room was unlike anything she had ever seen.

The room was a miniature museum. Lighted glass cases large and small held mementoes of years of hell-raising around the world. Some were serious and some were whimsical: Jennifer stared with fascination at a pair of gold lamé panties with the slightest hint of a stain at the crotch. The panties were encased in lucite, and a card told the story of their importance. It appeared that this particular pair were worn by Nikki the day on the tennis court when her tennis pro seduced her.

Jennifer stifled a whoop of laughter.

John Hamilton cleared his throat. "I thought if you saw this room you might get a better understanding of Nikki and Alain."

Jennifer held out her hand but changed her mind and kissed his cheek.

"Thanks for agreeing to talk with me, John. I've spent a lot of time day dreaming about the month we spent on your island. I've missed you all."

"Nikki and Alain were very disappointed—particularly Alain, I think—when you returned to New York. They don't meet many people they can romp with."

"Romp?"

"They're overgrown cubs, but cubs of a great lion, Père Mitya."

"Do you know him?"

"Yes. I'll tell you about him."

He stepped behind a bar in the corner of the room and she pulled up a tall stool and asked for a Perrier with a twist of lemon. She imagined Nikki and Alain sitting at the bar, chuckling over one of their "trophies."

"Do you think I could meet him, John? If you could get me in to see him, I'm sure I could convince him to let me take pictures."

John Hamilton shook his head and laughed.

"I know you're very persuasive, Jennifer, but you just don't understand. Père Mitya is one of the greatest living teachers. He has a reason for not wanting photographs of himself and his people. They can't do the work he sends them out to do if they attract publicity. The public wouldn't understand. The media has lied to it so much it's very confused."

"You mean all that about a sex cult? I don't go for that stuff, John. But who are these people who follow him?"

"Serious people, Jennifer. Men and women who have decided that they agree with Père Mitya that there are many different paths to the goal of enlightenment, that what works for one person may not work for the one next in line. They have chosen the path of sexuality."

"And the silver pin you wear? What does it signify?"

"Père Mitya's people are everywhere. It identifies us to each other."

"It looks like a tiny wheel. . . ."

"It's simply an 'O'—for the female vagina."

Jennifer sipped her Perrier and thought about what John Hamilton had said.

"Why don't Nikki and Alain wear the same pin?"

"Because they're his flesh and blood. The silver pin is earned by people who choose to enter the society of Père Mitya."

"And you?"

"My role? Père Mitya asked me to become their guardian."

"Their personal genie."

He chuckled. She liked his eyes when he was amused, how they sparkled as if at some private joke he was too reserved to share with her. She watched him pour a ginger beer and admired his graceful brown wrists.

"How would a photographer who would like to be permitted to cover Père Mitya—how would such a photographer go about earning one of those silver pins?"

"I can tell you about the silver pin, but earning one is difficult, and even if you do so there would be no guarantee that Père Mitya would allow you access he has strictly forbidden to many others."

"Have any of them earned the pin?"

"You are determined?"

"John, it's not just the pictures. It's Alain. I want to be up front about that."

She could feel John Hamilton's attitude change.

"But I don't understand. You might have stayed on the island with him. . . ."

"*And* with Nikki."

"Nikki?" He was puzzled. "You mean because they're brother and sister? He's sterilized, you know. Their intercourse is purely erotic. Without biological consequences."

"It's not that. It's just that I can't share him. I've never been able to share a man."

"Have you tried?"

"Yes—with my twin sister. We are very close, but it didn't work."

John Hamilton shook his head sadly. "That is too bad. Nothing and no one has separated them since they were children."

"I thought if I took pictures, if I could just be around him, then perhaps—"

"I understand." He had softened toward her.

"Help me, John." She touched his arm.

"I would like to. You're very charming, Jennifer. Very solid. I don't know if I can, though."

"Why not?"

"The people who earn the silver pin are sexual adepts. They had developed their erotic understanding long before they learned of Père Mitya's teachings."

"Well, I haven't exactly been shy about my urges over the years, John. I'd say I've kept up."

"Serial monogamous love affairs have nothing to do with the kind of erotic life represented by the silver pin—a life based upon freedom and imagination."

Shairoon had been standing near the bar listening to them. Her great dark eyes remained fixed on John Hamilton's face, as if she might miss something if she turned away.

"The woman needs help, John. Not fine speeches."

It was Shairoon's voice, but so unexpected that Jennifer looked for someone else in the room.

"What would you have me do?" John Hamilton asked Shairoon, making a point of being patient with her.

"Show her the mirrored room. See if she's still interested so much in Père Mitya."

"The mirrored room?"

John Hamilton explained. "Père Mitya is a practical joker. He got bored when he lived here and ordered that a mirrored room be installed in which he could "test" the sexual potential of some of his followers. Nikki and Alain used to have fun with it, after Père Mitya forgot he had it built."

"So did we," Shairoon laughed, crinkling her nose fondly.

"Come along. I'll show you."

It was a small room, perhaps 9 by 12, in which

## Book Five

mirrors covered the walls and ceiling. The floor was velvet-covered foam rubber.

Jennifer looked at the mirrors politely. She was puzzled.

"Maybe I'm not up to date, but I don't see. . . ."

"One of these mirrored walls is also a window."

"You mean people watching on the other side?"

"Or a video machine to record what happens in here."

"And what am I supposed to do in here?"

"Masturbate."

"Just like that? No build up, no music?"

He nodded. "Père Mitya's theory is that you can only be truly free in sex when you can free yourself from identification with your genitals. If I asked you to sit in this room and eat a meal, you'd have no difficulty doing so. Masturbation, sex itself, is in itself no more vulgar than mastication. In both cases body openings are satisfied."

"I don't think that I'm my cunt, John, but *I* want to decide who I display it to."

"Père Mitya would call that the 'sex is property' argument."

"Don't tell me you're going to make me do this."

"Try it. You'll have to go through worse trials than this if you want to see Père Mitya."

She waited for a minute after he closed the door. The mirrors gave her back reflections of her rather bemused countenance. Perhaps if she could hypnotize herself . . .

She picked up the hem of her green wrap and pulled it slowly up her leg, wondering, as she did, who was watching her. It was all right if she thought of John and Shairoon on the other side of the glass—after all, she had spied on their lovemaking on the beach—but not people she didn't know. Not a video recorder. She didn't want to see herself masturbating in full color on cable television.

"I can't," she confessed to the images of herself in the mirrors.

John's voice came over a microphone. "Why not?"

"It's too private. Can't I do something else?"

"Alain says your ass is exquisite. Pull up your skirt and show us."

"Do *you* want to see it? I'll show it to you, but not to strangers."

"Just pull your skirt up. Just pretend I'm the only one who's watching."

"I don't even know where you are! This is spooky."

She stood in the middle of the small mirrored room with her arms crossed protectively over her breasts. Her eyes were wide and her nostrils flared. "I'm a modest person," she protested to the mirrors. "Public displays are hard for me."

"Your WASP conditioning. It's not important. You have to shed it."

"But I don't understand how showing off my rear end is going to help me get beyond my conditioning."

"Simple. You've beaten your conditioning when you can be as casual and natural about displaying your ass as you are about letting people see your elbow."

Jennifer thought about this for a minute and decided that she wouldn't give John Hamilton the satisfaction of thinking she was uptight about her body.

She pulled open her wrap and held the material away from her body, exposing her curvesome cheeks, white where her bikini had covered them. She looked around defiantly.

"Well?"

"Beautiful. You have no *right* to hide such natural wonders. Now bend over so I can see the rest of you."

Jennifer blushed and dropped her skirt around her. John's vulgarity was unexpected, like a slap on the bottom.

"I won't do that, John. I refuse to degrade myself. I just won't step across that line."

"Degradation is what your culture says it is. In my country naked bodies are no different from naked trees, naked stones. Don't make a big deal of your ass—we all have one, don't we?"

What he said made sense, but words alone wouldn't be enough to make her feel better about displaying the most intimate secrets of her body. Her nakedness was to be presented like a gift to her lovers, not made available to everyone like a face on a coin. She wasn't public property.

Still, it was becoming clear to her that there would be personal benefits in undergoing the training required to earn the silver pin that went beyond pictures for *New Man* or a reunion with Alain. She was beginning to see that there were unexplored areas of her own sexuality. Dark places that she wanted to shine light on.

"You have to learn two things before I can send you to Père Mitya's ashram. You won't be ready for the O group until you learn how to become sexually independent, and how to disconnect your 'self' from your sex."

"How do I go about doing that?"

"You'll start with Vida Lancaster."

# 15

As a child Jennifer had touched her genitals the way she touched her tongue, or her navel. In the same play pen with her sister, they touched each other. Softness upon softness.

This hazy pastel memory of a sexual Eden was broken in Jennifer's mind by a sharply focused black and white interruption: her mother's firm reprimand when she'd caught Jennifer pushing two fingers in and out of the wonderful opening between her legs while lying in a bubble bath at the age of seven or eight.

"Jenny dear, that's not for you to touch. It's not polite."

At seven she hadn't understood why something that felt good and could be performed in private was wrong, but she trusted her mother, and thereafter masturbated only infrequently, behind locked doors. At the age of twenty-five she had only the vaguest idea of what her cunt looked like. The inward opening orchid of her womanhood was visible only to her lovers.

John Hamilton sent her to Windermere Farm in New Jersey, where a woman who wore the silver pin held weekend retreats for women who wanted to learn how to become sexually independent. This was Vida Lancaster, who was tall and angular and fair with intelligent eyes that saw everything you did. She spoke in urgent tones about everything and yet left an impression of herself as utterly calm and clear. When they did yoga postures, she was incredibly limber.

She presided over a light vegetarian lunch in a sunlit dining room. Jennifer sat at her right and three other women sat on her left. Vida cut bread for all of them, black, moist bread full of raisins. Jennifer had brought carnations that sat in a blue vase at the end of the oak table.

"What I have tried to establish here is a 'feminine community,'" Vida said. "A place where women come to express what it means to be sexually independent, and to learn about the beauty of their own sexuality. Women sharing their experience with each other."

A woman with a punk haircut spoke. "You're going to show us how to jerk off. Isn't that right?"

"You could say that—if you think you have something the rest of us don't have."

"Huh?"

"The first step," Vida said, "is to watch our language. We don't have anything to jerk off. We're not men and, as you will see, we are not dependent upon them for our sexual fulfillment."

After lunch they went to a large room with one glass wall through which they could see snowy farmland. There were mats on the polished oak floor, mats arranged in a circle for the five women whose clothes were scattered around the room. Their eyes glanced around the circle at each other and darted away.

Jennifer sat in a full lotus position and kept her eyes on Vida. Naked, Vida seemed less formidable. Her breasts sagged slightly and her knees were bony.

"I invite you to come on a trip with me, sisters," she began, sitting straight backed and proud like a priestess of Inanna, the Sumerian goddess of love. "This afternoon we're going to look at It together. You have your small mirrors, and you have everyone's permission to look in them. We are going to take a serious look at the source of life and the spring of human pleasure, from which all other pleasures flow. This remarkable organ, this nether mouth, this cunt, quim, cooch, snatch, yoni, pussy—is the center of your sexuality. Your sexuality was given you so that you can experience ecstasy."

Jennifer angled the mirror between her legs and looked at herself somewhat skeptically. Men liked her pussy, that was all that mattered, all she cared about. She liked their cocks, so it was a good trade. Did it matter that she felt just a little squeamish looking at her own genitals?

But . . . why did she?

She looked around. The other women were taking good long looks at themselves. Kathy, the woman with the punk haircut, lay back on her spine staring between her legs at the mirror with wide eyes.

## Book Five

Jennifer parted the soft blonde fur around her outer lips and used two fingers to open the inner lips. A pearly liquid oozed in the fresh pink. She had to admit that she liked the color—always had—but her outer lips seemed just a little too big. They marred her perfect beauty.

"Everyone's vaginal configuration is different. Go around and look at all of them. Don't think there's some kind of average you're supposed to conform to. And don't, above all, make the mistake of thinking yours is unattractive. It's first of all *you* who must be happy with it."

"My husband says I smell," a woman named Fern said. Her husband was a television producer who had no time for her.

"In relation to what? Chemical deodorants? If you wash, your natural smell is pleasant to the right person. Every good thing in life has its special smell."

"Maybe it's just *my* smell he doesn't like."

Two of the women crawled to her mat to look at her cunt. Jennifer joined them. Fern's sex smelled lovely to her. While she knelt before it, another woman smelled her. Soon all five of them were moving around on the mats examining each other like monkeys.

That night Vida showed them slides of female genitals. It was necessary, she said, for them to admire and understand the variety of vaginal forms. It was not solely functional, it was visually dramatic—beautiful, in fact.

One of the women tittered, and another joined her. They were sitting around on their mats in the meeting room sipping homemade elderberry wine, glad that the lights were off because their faces were flushing with embarrassment.

Kathy asked the obvious question. "Hey, I don't

go for women. Looking at pictures of snatch doesn't turn me on. I'm not queer. We've all looked at ourselves with mirrors, and we've looked at each other, and now these slides, but what I'm here to learn is how to be sexier with men."

Vida switched off the carousel slide projector and turned on the lights. Her rings clicked together when she brushed errant strands of lank hair from her forehead. She explained the philosophy of her workshops with passionate conviction.

"Kathy, you had never looked at yourself before. You were fascinated, I could see that. And I don't think that a woman can be a good lover unless she is fascinated by what brings her so much pleasure. I've discovered over the years, after working with hundreds of women, that the reason so many of them have experienced sexual problems is that they are not comfortable with their sexual organs. They've been taught not to look, not to touch, to be dependent on men for their pleasure.

"What we teach is how to become familiar and comfortable with your cunt so that you appreciate it and love it. Once you can do that, we teach you how to masturbate"—she paused to sip her elderberry wine—"not, of course, that you need to be actually *taught* how to do what comes naturally. All you need, in fact, is the permission to return to your childhood innocence, to recall how you stroked yourself before society shook its long finger at you. Once we give you permission to masturbate with a whole heart, as a primary source of self-gratification, you'd be surprised at the earthquakes you can cause between your legs, all by yourself.

"That's why we emphasize independence here. Masturbation is the key to full sexuality, because, as we see it, if you can't give sexual pleasure to yourself, you won't know enough about it to offer it to anyone else. I hope that answers your question, Kathy." She tossed her hair back.

To her credit, Kathy put her palms together and bowed politely. She had been given a lot to think about.

"Are there other questions?" Vida asked, looking around the room. Jennifer had been quiet, but when Vida looked inquiringly at her she spoke up.

"I've experienced some wonderful things today, but I still don't know if I can really do it. I mean, it's just such a struggle to overcome bad feelings about my genitals."

"I'm glad you spoke up, Jennifer. We all know you because of your reputation as a photographer, and, of course, your article in *New Man*. In a way, you are an American sex symbol, so if *you* have problems accepting your cunt, we know *something* is wrong."

All eyes were on Jennifer.

"It's just that I think you're right, and I wanted to say that. I masturbate, just like everyone else, but I always feel slightly ashamed of myself when I do it. Like I'm cheating or something. And I *never* look at myself."

Vida's warm smile was encouraging. "Go on," she said. "This is important for women to say."

"There's no more. I'm a photographer, not a talker. I *see* things and I go *snap*. It's hard for me to explain what it means to think that if I can play with myself I'm becoming a freer woman, but I think it's true."

"Would you do us a favor, Jennifer?"

"Well, I guess. . . ." What could *she* do?

"A demonstration—that's what's on tonight's schedule. Would you?"

"Would I what?"

"Demonstrate. Show us how you masturbate. Get up on that table by the windows"—she indicated the kind of table gynecologists use, complete with stirrups—"and just let yourself go."

"I . . . don't think I can do that."

"Why not? It's only us women. The point of the demonstration is that the more pleasure you give yourself, the more approval you get from your audience. We reinforce each other by taking turns on the table and in the audience."

Jennifer climbed on the table filled with trepidation.

Someone would laugh, she feared. Yet the women remained silent, fully respectful of her nerve in going first in an exhibition that none of them but Vida Lancaster had ever performed anywhere but in their gynecologist's office.

Not that they had masturbated for their doctors, but when Jennifer's splendid thighs were spread, and her feet placed in the metal stirrups at the bottom of the examining table, many of them were reminded of fantasies that had flitted through their minds while the doctor wielded his cold speculum.

They stood close around Jennifer, waiting for her to begin. She nervously stroked her thighs, letting her fingers circle her delta.

"Touch yourself, Jennifer," Vida urged. "Just as you did when you were a child."

Other voices were added to Vida's, and Jennifer was spurred by their encouragement to rub herself and fondle her breasts. Closing her eyes she conjured up Alain's image, wishing that he were here to nurture her lust.

As she continued to apply pressure to the source of her pleasure she lost her awareness of the people watching her. Their attentive eyes and excited breathing faded, and she knew that for the first time in her life she was going to be able to fly her own jet to wherever she wanted to go. Always before masturbation had been for relief of tension, secondary to male-female sex. Now she saw that she'd found a new lover. Herself.

Her jet had to lift from its runway heavy with preconceptions and warnings and thou-shalt-nots, but it lifted, and soon she was cutting through the upper stratosphere, hearing only the sound of her own powerful engines: the beating of her heart, the bellows of her lungs, the pounding of her stomach.

"Go, Jennifer, *fly!*" Vida Lancaster encouraged, and from somewhere in the roaring distance Jennifer could hear the other women cheering for her as she crested—and crested again—and again—each time under her own power.

# 16

"Would you mind taking care of my present now, honey?" Jennifer asked the stocky, seemingly shy man who hung back at the door of the bedroom. "It's our first time, after all. . . ."

The man gave her two fifty dollar bills folded together and stroked her palm with one finger when she took the money. She giggled obligatorily and turned her back to him so she could stuff the money in a bureau drawer. She wore a silk robe and heels.

The man was unsteady on his feet, but he was horny—my was he horny! When she'd seen him enter the spacious living room of the Park Avenue apartment where she had served three days as a priestess of Aphrodite—a call girl available to any man—Jennifer thought the man would be trouble. He had fire in him.

His face was strong but troubled. He was big, but it was muscle he was big with, not fat. He wore an expensive suit that was in bad taste and an absurdly defiant mustache that turned up at the tips. His first name was Adam, he said, adding an extra bite to the pronunciation of his second name. He was Armenian, he told her with moist eyes, an artist who made abstract drawings of women's bodies. For two years he had been self-isolated in a converted barn in Vermont, drawing breasts and asses that he saw only in his imagination. He was a passionate man with big hands who seemed to rumble with sexual expectations, and he had stoked his fire with rough brandy. He had come to her because he had not been with a woman in so long that it would be unfair to make love to an ordinary girl until he had slaked his pent-up lust.

Upon hearing that she had been so honored, Jennifer gulped appreciatively and led him to the luxurious bathroom with the sunken tub to which every client was guided before entering the bedroom. He stood obediently before the sink while she unzipped him and pulled out his long slender penis. She washed him with soap and warm water, making a seductive, teasing ritual out of a hygienic necessity. Often a man got so excited at this point he emptied himself into the washcloth.

John Hamilton had said that in order for her to learn to dissociate herself from her cunt she would have to prostitute herself. She would have to become a sexual object. Sex was a great storm and she had to understand that she was only one of millions swept up in it like dust motes; she did not direct her course in the storm.

He had piqued her sense of adventure, and she had accepted his challenge. When she looked around for a suitable temple in which to prostitute herself she thought of Misty, Jack August's friend. In addition to her work in films, Misty was something of an entrepreneur in flesh. She had a spot for Jennifer in her most active operation.

Jennifer was there to serve, to forget herself, her pride and her needs.

"What do you feel like, lover? Would you like me to rub your back, and get the kinks out of your legs?"

Adam nodded yes, his teeth bared gratefully. He strutted rather than walked to the brass bed and gingerly stretched across it. He'd had a lot to drink, but he was a big man with a strong determination to rut.

Jennifer shrugged out of her silk robe and stepped up onto the bed, squatting above his back and using her fingers and palms to flatten out the wrinkles between his shoulder blades and knees.

"You like that, lover?" she asked. The words came easily to her lips; she'd made love with eight strangers and earned in two days as much as she could make in an hour with her camera. She liked the variety of men she had met, but she didn't think she could afford to earn her living by prostitution. She had more expensive tastes than a call girl's income could support.

But, she smiled thoughtfully, now, she could see maintaining a few clients as a sort of hobby. It was kind of neat to have someone like Adam paying you a hundred dollars to match his sexual craziness.

He wriggled under her and she jumped up. He

leaned on one elbow on her bed and for a moment he reminded her of her favorite Uncle Mitch, with his thick mustache and watchful, toothy grin—as if just waiting for her to make a mistake.

She didn't like that image so she pulled him into her arms and moved her hands over his hard chunky body searching for the sensitive places, his erogenous zones.

"Do you like to be taken care of?" she asked.

"Oh yes," he said with certainty. "I do. I like you to ask me what I want. How I want it. Do I want the music a little softer, do I want a broader smile. . . . ?"

He touched her waist, and slipped his hand onto her breast. His fingers twisted her nipple, and she felt the answering signals of the nerves. It wasn't fair, she thought, that men could manipulate you like that. . . .

"Let me give your dick a kiss," she offered, nuzzling its tip. Clamping her hands around his muscular buttocks, forcing him against her face, tickling his balls. She knew what she was doing, having learned that what men really wanted was a woman who at least pretended that their erections were of great concern to her. Her role was to help create and protect any illusion her customers needed.

"I want all of you," Adam said thickly. "I'm a raging bull tonight."

"You paid for half and half, so let me suck you. I'll make it good."

"No, I want to eat you, like a fruit cocktail. I want to smear you all over my face, let your juices run down my chest. . . . Just lie back on the bed and put your legs up in the air. Split your legs and pull the lips of your pussy apart."

The way he talked got her more excited than she wanted to be. He was obviously going to hold nothing back from her, and she knew he was going to take his time. He was swollen with desire; his face was almost purple with it.

She did as he told her to, holding the outer lips of her vagina open with manicured fingers, showing him the ripe pink flesh buried between the long slender thighs she held apart and up in the air for him.

He began by kissing her in the hollows behind her knees and moving his open wet mouth up the soft satiny insides of her thighs. He stopped for a moment and when she looked at him saw that he was staring almost reverently at her wet groove, while he stroked himself.

"Suck me, honey. Put your big tongue right in my hole. Fuck my cunt with your cock tongue." The hot words came easily.

"You smell so sweet down here," he muttered from between her scissored thighs.

*I should,* Jennifer thought. The perfume she wore was $450 a bottle.

She ran her hands through her client's thick hair, shivering as she felt his long tongue stab into her again and again. She was afraid that Adam had been telling the truth about himself, that he was going to try to wear her out.

Waves of heat began to spread across her groin and up to her navel. His hands held her soft buttocks and his fingers stroked the groove between them. His little finger prodded the elastic ring of her rear opening, and then he inserted it up to the first knuckle. He pulled her to his face like a man eating a watermelon, making hungry, slurping noises that would have turned Jennifer off from a lover of her choice, but in this situation it just made her hotter. His noises were a tribute of a sort, after all.

She moved away from him when she felt the first signals of orgasm. He looked up from her crotch

*Book Five*

and smiled happily, his mustache and chin glistening with her juices.

"You taste as sweet as a peach and you burn my tongue, you get so hot. Your little hole is so small and so tight I'm afraid I might hurt you if I stick my Armenian dick in it."

"Put it *in* me, Adam. I don't care if it does hurt, you're driving me crazy. I want to feel that hard monster inside me." She giggled inside at the absurd dialogue, but it was true to the situation.

"Put it in for me then. I won't be responsible. Get yourself ready, because I'm going to fuck you so hard the tip of my dick is going to come out your throat."

His long slender penis jutted up from his belly, its swollen purple knob secreting pre-coital juice. She took it with both hands and pulled him on top of her, guiding his throbbing hardness into her wet sheath, encouraging him to press it into her, excited by his crude language, which she realized was a compliment paid to her desirability.

His shoulders were massive. He supported himself on well muscled arms above her, moving his hips slowly as he began to slip into her inch by delicious inch. She lifted her hips to meet him, encouraging him to bury the length of his penis inside her. She squeezed her pubic muscles and literally swallowed him, making him moan with delight.

"Oh you beautiful whore, it's as tight as your throat, I know it. It feels so good, so good, like you're sucking me off with your dear pussy."

She draped her legs over his shoulders and he pulled her ass off the bed and up into the air so that he could crash into her at the best and deepest angle of penetration. Her body shook with his onslaught. She held onto his shoulders and forearms while his stocky, muscular body banged into her ass and the backs of her thighs. He fucked her so hard and moved so rapidly that it was all she could do to hang on for the first few minutes. He plunged deep into her body, as if he might nail her hips to the mattress, sew her ass to the satin sheets. He attained a rhythm and held it, moving tirelessly while humming a bar of music she couldn't place. His eyes were shut and there was a look of perfect bliss on his heavy face. He was like a champion cyclist, a horseback rider, a swimmer—he had reached a certain plateau and he maintained it easily.

While he rode her he balanced himself on one hand and used his other hand to maul her firm breasts, squeezing them with such urgency that she didn't have a chance to complain before the same hand moved down to her flat belly and around to her ass. He squeezed the satiny half moons of flesh and then began to spank her lightly, to slap her with his open hand, like a rider lashing a mount to greater efforts.

She churned her hips, moving them up and down while breathing encouragement into his ear, as if she were trying to see how far this wild man could be driven. She was beginning to lose her bearings, coming close to the top of the highest roller coaster, trembling on the brink before plunging into orgasm. If she didn't get him off soon, she would be a wreck. So she made her words so obscene they burned holes in his consciousness.

"You're ripping me apart with that big club, lover. I can feel the love juice in your balls just waiting to shoot into me. Your balls are so heavy, so ready. Come on, drown me in your juice. Fill me up."

She felt the trembling begin in his arms and spread over his body uncontrollably, turning up in his calves and then his fingers, until at last his entire body vibrated like a rocket ship at launching.

She watched his eyes pop open. They bulged from their sockets. His tongue stuck out between his teeth and she could almost see steam coming out of his ears. Sure now that she would win their race, that he would come before the roller coaster started in her own body, she reached between his legs and caressed the base of his cock with two finger nails.

It took him over the edge. He looked surprised, and an involuntary groan escaped his lips. *"Ohhhh,"* he groaned again, and thrust into her with the force of a bull—thrusting again and again between her lifted thighs until the thick hot cream erupted from him and shot against her cervix two year's worth of stored-up desire.

Jennifer told Misty about Adam when they had lunch together in the kitchen of the Park Avenue apartment that afternoon.

"You can't do that, Jenny. My girls learn very quickly that if you let the customers use you that hard you'll end up too sore to sit down. You've got to remember that it's a whole lot easier on the system to give head to a guy like that."

"But he was enjoying himself so much. And he talked so dirty—I found it very arousing."

"They like that. That's part of our job, to let them get that dirty talk out of their system. Every good working girl knows that it's not the sex they come for, but the illusion."

"It's funny. I always thought it would be shameful to make love for money. It's still hard to ask to be paid for what you love to do, but I could understand feeling very good about being a call girl. This weekend I've been providing a real service. I'm a professional."

Misty sipped her coffee and munched a carrot stick. She wasn't impressed by Jennifer's discoveries.

"I still don't understand why you're doing this. You're a famous photographer. You don't have to turn tricks."

"I wouldn't have missed this experience for anything. I feel so good about myself. John Hamilton was right: I *do* feel more in control of my sexuality now that I've put some distance between it and me."

"Turning tricks is all right, sure, but I'd still rather be making love before a camera. Which reminds me—you promised you'd take pictures of me."

"I'll do it. I'll go home this evening, try to get some rest in, and then you'll come to my studio this week." Jennifer grinned. "Then you'll get to see how *this* working girl makes a living."

# 17

At last the day came when Jennifer was summoned to Père Mitya's new ashram in upstate New York. John Hamilton had called her: Alain and Nikki were back in the States, visiting their father. They had asked for her, and he'd told them what an apt pupil she had been.

So on an unexpectedly clear blue morning in early February Jennifer, wearing a sober wool polo coat and bluejeans and carrying only one large shoulder bag, took a taxi to Grand Central Station. In the huge main hall dominated by the Kodak display she bought a computerized ticket and ran to board a departing train. It would wend its way slowly up the east shore of the lordly Hudson, and bring her at last to the pleasant river town of Rhinecliff, where Alain and Nikki were to meet her with a car.

The train was almost empty, so she had a seat to herself where she could stare out the window at the passing landscape and try to get things straight in her head.

The past few months had been tempestuous. She had learned and grown. She was a different woman from the person who'd approached Nikki Armitage on sheer impulse and then surprised herself by following through on the chain of events activated by their meeting.

She rested her head on the back of the seat and closed her eyes. Thoughts and images flashed through her reflective mind, images on an inward screen that seemed to fall into three loose groupings:

—Did she really feel love for Alain? She *thought* she did, but she had been *sure* of it that night on the beach when she'd surrendered her ass to him. What was it about him that made him so exciting to her? She decided it was his ability to follow his nose to the next adventure—his spontaneity and impulsiveness.

But it was more than that. She thought she loved him because she couldn't figure him out, and because he . . . what? He smelled good? That was true. He had swept her off her feet? That, too, was true. It was a combination of things, but because she was a romantic she was fatally skeptical about love and reserved opinion on whether it had really happened to her or not. She'd felt such emotional flurries before, and none of them had worked out to her satisfaction.

—Her thoughts turned to the ashram which was at the end of her journey. She wondered what it would be like, and what she would be like in such an environment. From everything she knew, it was best to dress simply, so she had worn sensible wool instead of ermine, denim instead of her favorite material, silk.

She was especially curious about Père Mitya. It was difficult to imagine what Alain and Nikki's father would be like. This immensely charismatic, immensely wealthy spiritual leader was a legend. She wondered if she would be able to convince him to allow her to photograph himself and his followers. She felt prepared for him, but the question was: was he ready for her?

—And she thought about her experiences with Vida Lancaster and Misty's Park Avenue bordello. Masturbation and prostitution. Self and public, inner and outer, independence and coexistence—the two experiences were intense. They resonated in her mind. She'd learned what John Hamilton had been talking about, she thought: how to take responsibility for her own sexuality, so that she needed no one but herself; and how to cut the umbilical cord between emotions and sex, how to disconnect her heart from her cunt. She was more than the sum of her recent experience or desires—and less, perhaps, than she needed to be to face the next adventure.

Her head was still buzzing when the train stopped in Rhinecliff. She walked out of the storybook train station and gazed around the parking lot. She saw a gray Mercedes and walked across the asphalt toward it, crunching gravel and ice beneath her handmade boots.

She expected one of them—Alain or Nikki—to get out of the car to greet her, but it didn't happen. When she was five feet from the well-tended expensive car, its engine was started with a discreet cough.

She tried the handle on the front passenger door, and found it was locked. Nikki was at the wheel but she wouldn't open the door. Jennifer climbed into the back seat and Alain's lips came down hard on hers.

The transition was so abrupt between the real world of train stations and the magic world Alain and Nikki created around themselves that Jennifer rebelled for a brief minute, fighting against Alain's kiss. But he pressed down on her insistently and she had no choice but to surrender.

His tongue played inside her mouth and he unbuttoned her coat so that he could sneak his hand inside and touch her aroused nipples. His other hand pressed against the wrinkled denim of her jeans crotch, trying vainly to stroke her clitoris.

Nikki drove recklessly over the narrow country roads, slowing occasionally when a deer or a stray dog ran in front of the car and then speeding up again. She kept her eyes front after saying, "Hello, Jennifer. We missed you. Now we're really going to have some fun."

Jennifer held Alain at arm's length on the leather car seat. Looking at him made her feel good. She caught her breath.

"I've been wanting to do that for months. I haven't kissed any woman who kisses the way you do."

"Oh Alain, it's so good to be able to see you and touch you, and hear your voice. I left a part of myself on the island."

"So you'd have to come back for it?"

"I think so. . . ."

"I was sure you'd be back on the next plane. I put off going to Paris. You didn't come."

"I thought about it. That night on the beach has been replayed a thousand times in my mind. . . ."

"Then why didn't you come back?"

Jennifer hesitated to bring Nikki into it, then shrugged. It was the only way. She had to spell it out for him.

"Alain, I want more than one night in a lifetime alone with you! We were on the island for a month, and we had just one night alone. *One* night!"

Although she hadn't raised her voice, the effect of her statement—one she'd rehearsed for months in her mind—was as if she'd screamed. Alain turned forward and stared out the window. They drove past large horse farms and grand Hudson River estates and at last turned through stone gate posts onto ashram land.

# 18

Père Mitya's ashram was a low, rambling stucco building that sat on a gentle bluff overlooking the Hudson River. It had been a Dominican monastery for nearly a century and its design was ideally suited for Père Mitya's needs. Splendid scenery, isolation, an ample number of outbuildings, and a large main structure that had both single rooms for privacy and large public rooms for gatherings were the features that had prompted the shrewd Père Mitya to buy the property.

Alain took Jennifer to the narrow cell where she

was to sleep and excused himself. She couldn't tell what he was thinking.

"Maybe I'll see you at dinner this evening. I have to visit my father now. He's trying to teach me about business."

"When will I get to see him?"

"When he thinks you're ready, and not a minute before. 'It's all in the timing,' he always tells me. He may send a message to you. If he does, then do whatever he asks. It will be what he thinks you must experience before you'll be able to understand whatever he might tell you."

Jennifer nodded and sat down on the cot in her narrow cell feeling unsettled inside.

She lay back with her head propped on her hands and reviewed what she had learned about Père Mitya.

He was really a Russian prince—some even said a Romanov bastard, Anastasia's half brother—whose parents had disappeared with him before the Revolution. He had appeared in Afghanistan looking like a bandit and then had come west, striding with giant steps across the continent, stopping to study at the great universities in Germany and Italy, and to play a wicked game of cards in every resort frequented by the wealthy. His gambling winnings financed his career in the money markets, and then he'd taken it all and invested in land. He retired.

With his financial needs taken care of, Père Mitya had begun to attract small audiences for talks he gave on the revolutionary nature of eros. Soon he was filling halls with people who wanted to hear what the self-made millionaire had to say about spiritual matters and what he began to call 'the science of sexuality.' Like other radical teachers he gained a following among the disaffected young, and soon found that his ideas about sexuality as a path to enlightenment were being discussed all around the world. To escape the attention paid him he fled to the Himalayas, but that of course only added luster to his growing legend. He was a recluse when he returned to Europe, traveling about with a small band of adherents until he had settled at last in the United States.

The message that Alain had mentioned was delivered to Jennifer after dinner that evening. In the large hall a hundred men and women dressed in work clothes—the men with beards, the women with long hair—had eaten graciously and well. Their faces were open and honest, and some of them went out of their way to make friendly overtures to her, but she didn't understand these people. They formed a community and she was an outsider.

The message was left next to her plate. It was typed on a blue index card.

*"There is one more step you must take. One more level before you break."* Break? She furrowed her brow. One more level?

Alain did not appear. She went to her room alone and turned the lights out early.

Jennifer didn't sleep well in her narrow bed that night. Perhaps it was her Yankee caution that kept her tossing and turning. She wondered with the acuity of three A.M. if perhaps she had stepped over the line at last, if this time she had gone too far in pursuit of a love affair and a stunning photograph. Her panic button throbbed like a sore tooth.

She could be sitting in her apartment watching tugboats on the river. She didn't have to be lying awake in a monastery by herself wondering what the morning would bring.

It seemed like she'd been asleep for only five minutes when she felt a tickling at her eyelids. She shook her head and saw Alain grinning at her, his face distorted because it was so close, saying "wake up." He'd been kissing her eyes.

She reached for his hand and put it on her breasts, but he pulled away. She fumbled for her Rolex on the nightstand. It was five A.M.

"Alain! The roosters aren't up yet!" she protested, but Alain put his finger up to his lips to stop her complaint.

"Get dressed." She pulled on her blue jeans and a sweater against the morning chill.

"I'm not even awake," she yawned.

"That's why the group begins so early. When you first awaken your defenses are down. You can be reached."

"What kind of group?" she asked, following him down the corridor, hurrying after him.

He explained it to her over his shoulder. "It's called the O group, after the silver pin."

"What does it stand for? Orgasm, I suppose."

"No. That's trite. It stands for openness. Openness is the key, my father says—openness and trust."

The O group. Participation in the famous O Groups at Père Mitya's ashram was limited to people the guru thought might become true sexual masters, usually only a half dozen at a time. Getting through this group was such an ordeal that it had been compared to running an Iroquois gauntlet.

The idea was simple: To rip away every layer of deceit and subterfuge about the erotic impulse built up in the individual by societal conditioning, it was necessary to undergo a rigorous deconditioning. Every preconception had to be reexamined.

Jennifer sat in the middle of a ring of six naked people on a rough gym mat. The walls around the large room were padded with the same material. They were gray and rough and stained with previous O Group encounters.

The room smelled like a gym because of the odor of perspiration, but there was also an unmistakable musky odor of sex that seemed especially sharp to Jennifer, although perhaps that was because her nose was still waking up, and took everything too seriously.

She looked around the naked circle and saw Alain sitting cross-legged whispering something into Nikki's ear. The other four people were about her age—three men and a girl, whose name, she learned, was Nicola. Nicola's burned out eyes made her uneasy.

"Good morning," she said nervously.

She was reassured by Alain and Nikki's presence in the room.

"You start, Jennifer," Alain said. "Just start talking."

Maybe it was the hour, but they looked grim, like a jury of people who had already made their decision—and nothing she said would convince them differently.

"I guess you know," she told them, "that I took Vida Lancaster's workshop. I spent a weekend offering myself to any man who happened along. I'm twenty-five, and I've been running on the fast track. Don't talk down to me."

"What about love?" Nikki asked.

"I love Alain. I wouldn't be here otherwise." Jennifer's answer was quick, definitive. Her glance around the room was defiant. She thrust her chin up, displaying her fine elegant neck. Let them talk about love; it was her subject.

"But you also want to be permitted to photograph

us—Père Mitya's happy children." Nicola was lightly sarcastic.

"It's my way of understanding what I experience. My camera is an extension of me—a sexual organ perhaps."

"I think it's your way of hiding, Jennifer," Nikki said.

"Oh, Nikki. . . ." There was so much she couldn't say to the small, exotic woman. She turned her head away.

Later Jennifer decided that the O Group was probably the single most important experience of her life. These six people knew her better than she knew herself. If she said "I can't do *that*," she was shown how to.

The first hurdle was display.

They'd talked all morning, stopped for a light lunch, and then Alain, as group leader, announced the first exercise of the week they would be spending together. Dozens would follow that were more difficult, but this was the first step across the line.

Display. Self-exposure. She simply didn't go for it, which was why she'd kept her skirts down in John Hamilton's mirrored room, why being blindfolded and naked before Alain had impressed him so searingly into her emotions, and why despite her beauty she felt uncomfortable in front of the camera. Why she had chosen—perhaps Nikki was right—to hide behind the camera.

Of course Alain knew this. She saw the mischievous look in his eye when he returned her stare. He looked almost boyish when he spoke, a sexual Huckleberry Finn.

"We've talked this morning about ourselves and how we've attempted independently to decondition ourselves. The programs we've gone through, the seminars, the conferences. Our experiences with love and sex. We've talked and we've talked and we have said enough. Talk won't put us in touch with ourselves. Or with each other.

"We're going to spend some intensive time together for the purpose of shedding all the notions we've acquired about sexuality. It will be painful and perhaps even dangerous, because in here anything goes, short of deliberate physical injury. The rules are simple: you can leave anytime you want, but you cannot come back once you've left."

He looked into each person's face to make sure he was understood.

"You've talked about yourselves," he said. "That was easy. Now you're going to show yourselves in your flesh. Who wants to start?"

Jennifer glanced around the room to see if anyone looked as nervous as she felt. Nicola was pinning up her long dark hair with deft, flashing hands, as if preparing for hard work. The three men were impassive. They were all in their thirties and none of them were conventionally good-looking. One looked like a small-time hoodlum, or an out-of-work actor. His face was unlined but his hair was prematurely gray and swept back from both temples like wings. Jennifer sensed that his body was going to tell her more about him than what he'd said during the morning—which was that his name was Monte.

"How about you, Jennifer?" Alain asked.

"What is it that you want me to do?"

"Introduce yourself to everyone in the room without saying a word. Use your body and your sexuality."

"How far should I take it?"

"Just as far as you can."

"How long?"

"Take your time."

She thought, but didn't say, *that was what I was afraid of*. He had made it clear that she would have to prove herself to him, that in the group there was nothing between them.

She swallowed and wondered if she could request a blindfold.

Quickly, she considered her options. There seemed to be only two if she was to overcome her stubborn modesty. She had been able to display herself with total freedom in only two situations: when she made love to someone special, and when she was blindfolded.

She shut her eyes tight. That felt better. She could pretend she didn't have an audience. She could think about what to do.

"Jennifer? Are you still with us?"

Jennifer opened her eyes. She couldn't hide. They were all looking at her expectantly, or mockingly, as in Nicola's case. She had no camera to hold up to distract them. They gave her their full attention.

The man named Monte licked his lips and she saw that he had bitten them. Was he as nervous as she was? She would start with him, then. She would show herself to him, and block the rest of them out. To him alone she would offer her gifts.

But first she knelt before him and bowed, letting him feel the full force of her bright blue eyes, the reality of the woman behind them. His dark pupils were hard and commanding, and he regarded her with the calm gaze of the animal trainer. She read in his face that women did not impress him, and that he was immune to the softening effect of beauty such as Jennifer's, but she read it too late.

She was kissing him, her lips barely touching the bruised skin, just brushing his lips really, getting his attention.

Sitting back on her knees, she crossed her arms and pulled her turtleneck over her head. The motion thrust her breasts out; they jiggled temptingly before Monte. Her nipples were strawberries that he could imagine between his teeth.

Women loved Monte because they could see themselves in every corner of his being. Yet he was disdainful of them. He was disdainful now of Jennifer's first offering, and she sensed it.

She blushed and pushed her blonde hair away from her face with both hands. Monte looked at her breasts and wanted to squeeze them hard, to press them together around his erection, but still he was disdainful. Half the population of the world was female—the supply of breasts was plentiful. Jennifer Sorel, big-time photographer, would have to do more than show him her chest before he acknowledged the gifts she offered.

His arrogance was a challenge. Maybe his laid-back approach worked wonders with less discriminating women because they didn't call his bluff, but Jennifer was about to.

She was uncomfortably aware that Alain and Nikki were watching her. Nicola and the two other men didn't matter so much, but she thought she would be embarrassed if Alain saw what she was going to do. She wasn't even sure that she could bring herself to do it, but if she did and Alain saw her—well, that was just the point of this exercise, wasn't it? Exposure. Opening up.

Whatever that meant.

To her it meant becoming more animal than human, making herself smaller by reducing her complex personality to this or that bodily appetite. On the other hand, she knew that her attitude was the product of a privileged existence, and careful cultural conditioning.

## Book Five

She stood up and stepped out of her blue jeans, wriggling a bit to peel them over her plump bottom, standing on one leg to pull them off, without taking her eyes from Monte's face. He sat at her feet, close enough to touch her.

Naked, Jennifer was more beautiful by far than any woman Monte had seen. It was in his eyes. He blinked rapidly, but she saw the appreciative glint in the obsidian glances he cast at her long legs and round bottom. Stretched to her full five feet seven, she towered over him, standing still as a newly carved sculpture while he admired her with the wonder of a rough man who has just discovered art—a man upon whom it is dawning that the women he has known before her were crude Roman copies of an exquisite Greek original.

His disdain had left him, and his admiring gaze was a silent salute to her beauty. Like a cat watching a mouse, he watched her breasts and the triangle of Venus between her thighs. Heartened by this sudden change in his attitude, Jennifer pivoted to let him enjoy the curves of her buttocks and the soft china of the backs of her thighs. She posed for him alone and closed her eyes to the rest of the room, the silent observers.

She was lost in a kind of reverie that she'd wrapped around herself like a cloak when he touched her, when she felt his hard fingers stroking her calves, cupping the firm muscles and moving up to her knees, his thumbs in the hollows behind her knees. She resisted the intrusion of reality into her dream state by kicking her leg free; at last she had been able to hypnotize herself into standing naked in a room of strangers, and she was enjoying her exhibitionism.

He clasped his hand firmly around her ankle. She looked down at him and tried once again to pull free. First he had ignored her, and now he was trying to tether her.

She could see why the O group training was reserved for Père Mitya's hand-picked candidates and not open to the public. She had the sinking feeling that she could get into a lot of trouble in this little room—and that Alain might not intervene.

This man was bothering her, damn it! She wasn't used to being annoyed with such persistence. His hands were touching her thighs, and then he performed some kind of trick behind her knees and she fell down into his lap. It was all against her will, and she struggled against him until he let her go. She rolled away from him and rested against the opposite wall. Monte glared at her, his anger adding fuel to his arousal.

"Well, Jennifer?" Alain's voice called her back to reality.

"Yes?" She had to clear her throat.

"We have time this afternoon for another exercise, which might fit in with what you and Monte are doing now."

"Alain, I'm not *doing* anything with Monte. You told me to do that first exercise and I got into it. Monte is a guilty bystander, as far as I'm concerned."

Alain sat down beside her. "Look, Jennifer. You've got to throw yourself into it. You have to go all the way. No holding anything back." He stroked her hair gently as he spoke.

"All right. What should I do? I really want to do this, Alain. You know I'm trying."

"Work through what you started with Monte. Learn what you can from that."

"But why can't I do that with you?"

"Because there's a lot of aggression in you about sex that has to be worked out, and I don't want to get knocked down in the fracas. Monte is an ideal match for you at this point: he irritates you, and you irritate him. The rest of us in the O group can watch you two go at it and learn a lot from the spectacle."

"Thanks, pal." She grimaced.

"Jennifer, if you can't do it you can leave," he said firmly.

Did he want her to fail? The thought added to her uncertainty about what to do next. It crossed her mind that perhaps the O group was a test that none of his girlfriends ever passed, that he used it to screen them out so there was never any competition for Nikki.

She shook her head. She shouldn't think such thoughts. Nikki was a dear friend—beautiful, charming, adventurous, sexy—but irrevocably *extra*.

She knew what she was going to do when she turned back around to face Monte, who had taken off his clothes and stood with his face half in shadow against the wall.

Her course was set. She would get through O group and be granted an audience with Père Mitya and earn the silver pin of the sexual adept—all because she wanted Alain to herself, all because she wanted to understand the nature of his attraction for her, *why* she felt compelled to do these crazy things for him.

Prepared as she thought she might have been for the sight of a naked Monte, her jaw dropped when she saw the enormous penis that lay on his thigh as if he'd had an extra hand to rest there. She had known men with large organs, but Monte's was mythic in proportion. She felt a cramp in her lower abdomen. So *that* was the secret of his laid-back success. . . .

She sat down on the mat before him, patting the space next to her.

"Come sit," she invited. Her smile was wide and

friendly. She wasn't even conscious that she was naked, she was so determined to bring this man into her orbit.

He sat beside her with his face turned away. His sideburns were romantic, she thought. The gray was premature, for he was a young man. He no longer looked like a small-time hoodlum to her.

"You liked looking at me, I could see that."

"You liked showing yourself off, didn't you?"

"It was awkward for me. That's why I kicked. I don't like being held down. I'm very independent."

He laughed as if he didn't believe her, short and derogatory. He was English, with the Midlands accent.

"It's true," she protested.

"You're independent? With a body like that? No, some man's got a hold on you. I can see you're already taken."

"That's not true."

"He's here in this room. It's Alain. You're eating your heart out for him and that's why you're here."

"Leave Alain out of this. It's my choice."

He relapsed into silence, thinking his own thoughts.

"You're really big, you know," she told him. "I've never seen anything quite so big on a man."

"Women like it," he agreed. "I've had some good —and bad—experiences because of having something its size tucked away."

"Is size really that important?" she asked.

He snorted. "Don't ask me. You're female. Are big tits important? You tell me."

"I guess so."

"Do you want to touch it?"

"Yes, but then it would get complicated."

"No. You can touch it. I'm able to control myself."

Jennifer giggled throatily. She felt like she was about ten years old and in her father's basement playing doctor. She stretched out her hand and touched first the hard, muscled ridge of his thigh and then the soft firmness of his penis.

At twenty-five years of age Jennifer could say with assurance that she had encountered just about every kind of penis born of woman, but never one quite so generously proportioned. Her fingers closed on it as if taking measurements, because she couldn't believe that she could tickle a man's balls at one end of a caress and have to take a break in between so that she might complete the caress convincingly on the other end of his shaft—a massive corona that was slowly becoming engorged with blood as her fingernails tickled it.

*What a weight,* she exclaimed to herself. *What am I doing playing with it? This thing can't go inside me. I must be crazy. Such a connection is impossible.*

She hefted the weight of his desire in her fingers. When she felt a fluttering she took her hand away. He was hard, but all she'd done was to satisfy her curiosity—how could she be blamed for that?

Perhaps if he'd bent his long neck—which seemed as stiff as his penis at the moment—to kiss her waiting lips Monte would have found Jennifer as receptive as some of the other women who'd worshipped his phallus.

They regarded each other for a moment like enemies. He was a man who was accustomed to having women fawn over him because of the size of his penis, and she was a woman who had always been able to pick her men like a gardener cutting flowers.

Never in her life had she given a moment's thought to penis size except to think occasionally how nice it was that things fitted. It had always been the total man that had turned her on. His voice, his smell, the way he talked to other people, how considerate he was of her. Sex had never been reduced to organ size, to sheer quantity of flesh.

"I know what you're thinking," he said to her. "It's just too big."

She laughed. Of course it wasn't that.

"That's what I think," he assured her. "I think *you* think it's too big. But it's not, and I'm going to show you. You'll see: it won't be bad. You'll wonder why there isn't more when you get used to feeling it inside you."

"You're kidding, of course."

"Oh, no. Feel this. Just feel how hot it is. Feel *that*!"

Jennifer cringed inside, seeing where everything had led her. Oh, no. His long club was banging against the side of her thigh.

Jennifer moved away from him, scraping the soft skin of her buttocks on the canvas mat. "No," she objected to him.

"Yes," he insisted to her. He moved quickly, pinning her wrists to the mat and covering her legs with one of his. She was always amazed at how heavy men were. Their legs, for instance, weighed tons—she couldn't wriggle out from under Monte's.

She struggled in vain to keep her legs together, but he was strong and insistent and pulled them apart like popsicle sticks, ramming between them impatiently.

"Don't do that!" she cried in vain.

"*Now*," he seemed to grunt above her, "I want you to relax. Just relax every muscle below your waist, or else we won't be able to do this."

Stunned, Jennifer felt him drive his stiff flesh against her pubic mound.

"But I don't want to!" she protested, thrashing her legs against his superior strength, thrashing them

## Book Five

until he caught both and knelt poised above her to deliver the goods, no matter how she protested.

He was slow and deliberate, but he pushed between her legs and was approaching the prize when she bucked her hips and threw him off.

"You're trying to rape me!"

"They all say that at first."

"I don't want to fuck you, man, I really don't. Get off me!" She twisted her body in violent protest.

"Just relax, like I said. This thing is so hard, honey, I don't know what will happen. You just kept touching it. . . ."

She knew he was serious and it didn't seem that there would be any way to match his superior power.

"Alain! Please call him off!" she pleaded.

Alain didn't react, nor did she hear anyone else responding to her cry for help.

She wasn't ready for him. She tried to crawl away but he held her fast. He was intent on jamming his giant thing between her legs, stabbing her hungrily and ruthlessly. Taking her without the slightest regard for whether or not she wanted him inside her.

*Ohhh,* she groaned. He had breached the first line of resistance, the dryness of her tissues, and was prodding into her as if welcome. She felt her insides clench tight against this invasion and she beat her clenched fists against his back. She didn't cry out because she knew no one would help her. This was her struggle. The giant rod of flesh ramming into her belly had no real connection with her feelings. She would fight it in every way she knew.

One of these ways was to use her pubic muscle and the strength of the vaginal muscles to force him to finish quickly. If she couldn't expell him, she could make him sputter out.

But he stroked into her with no regard for her

counter-pressures. For all her tensing against him he moved like a metronome. When she started rocking her pelvis back and forth in the hope of tossing him from her body, he grinned and dug his heels in.

"Get—off!" she panted, pushing at him, her eyes blazing.

"You like it," he told her. "I know you like it."

"I don't like it—and I can't stand you!" she responded. She lifted her fingers to scratch his eyes and then dug them into his back instead, fearing the punishment of his hands.

*This was what the note had meant*, she thought. *"One more level before you break."*

He *was* too big for her, but that wasn't the problem. If she had wanted him, working together they might gently have stretched her. The problem wasn't the sensations being caused by his monstrous organ as it filled her insides, for after the initial friction against dry membranes she had lubricated quickly enough. The problem was that he was forcing her. He wasn't brutal but he overcame her resistance by superior power, holding her so she couldn't move.

Jennifer was a sexually experienced woman. Men had used her roughly before—most of them only once—and she knew that Monte wouldn't hurt her if she didn't resist, that all she had to do was wait until he was finished. But she wouldn't give him the satisfaction of taking the old when-it's-inevitable-lie-back-and-enjoy-it attitude. Even if it did feel good she wouldn't let him know it—and it wouldn't feel good. Rape would *never* feel good.

But she didn't expect him to plead with her.

"Please move your body. I must feel you."

"No."

Knowing how much he wanted her cooperation made her even more determined to fight him with passive resistance, to make her body limp and dead to him. She closed her eyes and pretended that she was in the Yogic corpse position, imagining the center of her being deep inside her, so that what was happening to her body was like something buffeting the walls of a house she sat in.

He was shaking her. "Don't do this to me," he begged. "Help me just a little bit, please, you're so beautiful. . . ."

She shook her head because she knew that she'd won. He was shrinking inside her and he wasn't going to be able to come. At last he stopped moving on her body and simply collapsed on the mat next to her, his long penis like a crumpled horn on his thigh.

## 19

"What do you want to do to Monte, Jennifer?" Alain held her safe in the circle of his arms.

"I don't know."

"Aren't you angry?"

"You bet I am." She pushed her face against his chest.

"Are you hurt?"

"Only my pride. Dignity. Those things."

"You must want to pay him back. It's only natural."

"I knew what I was getting into, Alain."

"You're taking this too calmly. Everything is bottled up inside."

"I was trained to control my feelings."

"Tell me the truth: What would you really like to do to Monte?"

"What do you want me to say, Alain? That I'd like to do to him what he did to me?"

He shrugged. "Why not? It would serve him right."

All she really wanted was for him to take her off alone someplace in the ashram and hold her for a long time, but she knew she couldn't say that.

"You're not opening up, Jennifer," Nikki said. She was joining Alain in his attempt to bring Jennifer face to face with her fury by goading her into a genuine response.

"You were raped, Jennifer. *He* did it, and he's right there," Nikki said, pointing an accusing finger at the prone man.

"I have the right thing for him," Nicola said, pulling from a capacious bag a large black rubber dildo attached to a leather harness.

Jennifer gaped at the apparatus, allowing her imagination to create some vivid *tableaux* in which it played a central role.

"Put it on," Nicola urged her. "Fuck him with it."

Monte was staring at her when she looked in his direction. His mouth was disdainful again. He'd heard Nicola, and he dared her to do it.

She wondered if she had the courage.

"Don't think about it," Nikki whispered. "Just do it. Do *exactly* what you feel like doing for a change."

Jennifer nodded. She would do it. Nicola helped her fix the leather harness around her waist and hips and she was able to bounce the long black rubber penis up and down. It was flexible and yet hard, like a blackjack. A weapon. In a flash she understood something about male *macho*—that it was a responsibility to carry such a concealed weapon around with you.

Nikki and Nicola were both small women, but they jumped on Monte like Amazons, pinning his arms to the canvas mat. He rolled back and forth a bit, but he didn't put up much of a fight. His large body lay passive, pinioned.

"He wants it," Nicola said. "I think he wants it."

"Now, Jennifer," Nikki said. "He won't move."

"I can't do it this way."

"Why not?"

"It will hurt him. There's no lubrication."

"In my bag," Nicola said, pointing. Jennifer found a jar of vaseline in her bag and rubbed the dildo with it until it was shiny. She knelt over her rapist's body, her hands on his tight, muscular buttocks.

He cried "no" in a faint voice which the women ignored.

Jennifer's fingers pulled his cheeks apart—they were covered with fine dark hairs, very *macho*—and exposed the tight rosebud in the center of the dark, damp crease. She could smell the mixture of perspiration and sex that clung to his hairy scrotum.

"Stick it in, Jennifer, go ahead," Nikki said.

The three women knelt over the prone, naked man like angels of vengeance. Their faces were set angrily as they bent to the task of violating the violator.

Nikki reached for Jennifer and kissed her on the mouth, imprinting her intensity. Jennifer inserted her little finger in Monte's anus and withdrew it when she felt the answering pressure.

"*Now*, Jennifer!" Both Nikki and Nicola called, and she pushed the tip of the black dildo into the small round target. He moved and the dildo slipped out, but she pushed it back in, helped by other hands.

She drove into him at least two inches and heard him scream. He thrashed for a minute and it was all the two women could do to hold his powerful legs.

Jennifer exulted. Now *she* was the conqueror, now he would feel what she'd felt—the helplessness, the shattering of pride.

The anger came tumbling out of her as she pushed the long black dildo deep into Monte's ass, pushed it in and pulled it almost out, then pushed it all the way in to its eight inch hilt. The rhythm of being the one doing the fucking captivated her. So *this* was what men felt! This feeling of dominance, of steering the ship, that you experience staring down at the naked buttocks of the person who was satisfying your desires.

She plunged into him with the same vehemence he'd shown when he raped her. She wished she had a nerve connection between her clitoris and the black dildo so that she could experience for herself the tightness men always talked about. She had to imagine it based on the resistance the dildo met with, how the anus tried to keep it inside.

"I hope you feel it, you bastard!" she said as she moved the dildo in and out of Monte's ass. "I hope your ass hurts the way my cunt did, but more important, I hope you understand what you did to me. You raped Jennifer Sorel, a person with a high regard for herself and her independence. You made me feel like I had no control over my own sexuality, which is very special to me. I came here to learn how to open up what's supposed to be repressed, and you reminded me very fast *why* I was conditioned to repress showing my body off."

"What do I want to *do* to you?" Jennifer continued, her rage growing as she thrust the glistening black dingus into him, feeling herself graced with an extra charge of energy so that she was able to zap it to him tirelessly as she vented her anger. "What do I want to do to you? I want to teach you that a woman isn't a tissue to be used, and discarded when when you feel horny."

She rode hard into him and he twisted his face around on the mat so that he could see his three captors.

"You asked for it. You teased. . . ."

"I suppose I did. I was told to, but you're right: I teased you. Just the way a little kid teases the lions between the bars at the zoo, I guess. You couldn't restrain yourself."

"Your beauty made me forget everything. . . . I didn't expect it. I've always been able to control myself. It was you—I swear it was just you. I'm not a rapist."

She didn't believe his line. She thrust into him again and felt satisfaction when he groaned.

"Do you like taking it in the ass, Monte?" Nicola asked, leaning down to breathe the question in his ear, then repeating it in a louder, more vengeful voice.

The question seemed to be the final straw. From somewhere he gathered his energy and roared, rearing up to send the three women tumbling away from him. Jennifer felt the harness around her hips jerk as the dildo slipped out of his ass.

He rose to his feet like an angry god, bearing his fully erect penis in both hands, holding it like a farmer pulling up a huge root.

"How did *that* happen?" Nikki said. Jennifer looked at Nicola, who shrugged. What had they done?

"There it is!" he shouted at them. "You don't know what it's like to be cursed with such a thing? I get in trouble with it wherever I go. Women make challenges. Men make jokes. I wish I had the nerve to cut it off and become something else."

His words were so sincere, spoken with such eloquent passion, that Jennifer felt moved—and confused yet again.

"Why did you rape her?" Nikki asked. "Don't tell us your prick made you do it."

He fell on his knees in front of the three women. Only by an occasional glance over their heads was it apparent that he was also addressing Alain and the two men who had so far watched without saying anything.

"This flesh of mine is an albatross. When I was a boy it was already this big. The girls started lining up by the time I entered high school. Can you blame a man for being foolish when so much attention is paid to something he had nothing to do with? Look at me. I'm an ordinary-looking guy. Nothing special. But when I take off my pants the women come around like I should be a great lover. It wasn't *my* fault they came around and expected so much, but they did. And even if I wasn't much good, they didn't seem to notice, or maybe they just didn't care. It was something they could tell their friends, like a guy telling his buddies about laying the girl with the biggest tits in town."

"You learned, didn't you?" Jennifer asked. "Didn't you learn that women know how to *ask* for what they want?" Her tone was sharp, but she was beginning to feel a great deal of sympathy for Monte.

He shook his head. "No, all I learned was how to treat women like they treated me. They were objects. Interchangeable. I could have who I wanted and it didn't mean a thing. They didn't want me, they wanted my cock."

Nicola laughed bitterly, although it was obvious

from her eyes that she too had been affected by his story. It was a story that any woman could identify with because if she herself didn't have large breasts, a friend did.

"But you don't have to go around raping women, you know," Jennifer countered.

"I told you, I couldn't help myself when I saw you. I apologize for that, because as soon as I saw your body I knew I would do anything to have you."

"And you did," she reminded him. "What's your ass feel like?"

He reached behind him and pursed his lips, finding the damage. "It's sore."

"Just like my cunt."

They grinned at each other ruefully. Nikki and Nicola sat watching them, waiting for something to happen with more than normal interest. They had taken off their clothes and Jennifer knew that they hadn't stripped just to continue an interesting conversation about how miserable sex objects could feel. They were announcing their readiness to play.

Well, why not? One look at Monte's oversized ten inch organ and it was obvious that there was more than enough room on it to support them all. She saw Nicola's dark ringed eyes glittering with impatience to jump on Monte. Nikki was more reserved, but she too had her almond gaze fastened on Monte's swollen penis.

Jennifer stepped out front. She certainly had first claim on Monte. She had suffered, and she had earned her reward.

Delicately, like a Japanese geisha, she bowed between Monte's legs and put her lips around the mushroom head of his giant stalk. Her tongue played in the slit there and tasted an answering fluid that translated itself into happy nerve endings around her clitoral area. Sucking turned her on, especially when she had the chance to take such an extraordinary male blossom in her mouth.

Both hands moved up and down his thick, swollen shaft as she sucked, moving the loose skin over the veins and pleasure bumps. Her cheeks were bloated with it.

She took her head away when she saw how much Nikki wanted to finish the job she'd started, how wet Nikki's small mouth had become in anticipation of taking Monte between her lips.

"You can have him, Nikki," Jennifer said, surrendering her position from between Monte's legs and watching as Nikki bent to her pleasant task.

Nicola was realistic. She knew Nikki wouldn't be finished for a long time, so she began touching the two men left in the room besides Alain. She knew that Jennifer had a claim on the O group leader.

Alain gave Jennifer the congratulatory salute of a man who doesn't quite believe what he has seen transpire before his own eyes. Behind them an orgy was in progress, but they embraced as if they'd never touched before.

Jennifer kissed Alain long and lovingly, attempting to pack into her kiss all the feelings of the group encounter—everything that she had been missing.

When their lips parted, Alain told her that the most important encounter was to happen immediately.

"My father wants to see you," he said.

"Now? Can't it wait?"

"Apparently not. He says timing is everything."

## 20

PERE Mitya made it a strict rule never to see more than one person at a time, and what he said in these private audiences was specific to the individual. Père Mitya was not interested in mass movements.

Alain brought her to his father's private bungalow hidden in a corner of the ashram property away from the main building. It was a chilly night; there was a fog rising from the river.

They stopped outside the nondescript house and Alain put his arms around her, pulling her close to him so that he could feel her breasts under her polo coat. He had something to say to her, and struggled to find the right words.

"Jennifer, I want to tell you something. I can't find any reasons not to fall in love with you. It was real—on the island."

She stood on tiptoe to kiss him. Afraid that if she said anything the emotional intensity might frighten him, she simply whispered in reply, "Yes, it was."

He turned and walked off, leaving her alone. She listened until she could no longer hear his footsteps on the cold ground. She took a deep breath, expelling icy clouds into the air, and knocked on the plain door of Père Mitya's private bungalow.

The door was opened a stingy, heat-conserving crack and a medium-sized man with a white beard stuck his chin out.

"Yes?" His *s* hissed. She couldn't place the accent.

"I'm Jennifer Sorel. I have an appointment."

"Oh, I remember. Come in."

She stepped inside the door and found that it was dark except for the moonlight that seeped in one window near her. The bearded man made big eyes at her, followed the gesture with a *namaste*, and crooked his finger.

She followed him through a large dark room that seemed populated with sleeping cats. She stepped over them with remarkable luck and stopped when he turned on a light above a kitchen table.

A Tiffany lamp of swirly green and amber designs provided the kind of dim light that feels best to the eyes late at night. It hung over a white enamel kitchen table on which sat a two pound jar of peanut butter, a crumbling hunk of dark, moist pumpernickel bread, and a large knife.

The man with the white beard sat down at the table and picked up the knife. He used it to cut two hunks of bread and held one of them up to Jennifer.

"Hungry?"

"I'm looking for Père Mitya. Are you him?"

"What do you want to know?" he asked.

He looked up at her from under bushy white eyebrows and smiled one of the most wonderful smiles Jennifer had ever seen. He used the knife in his hand to spread buttery brown over the moist black bread, and then put the confection in his mouth. His teeth were large and white, and made short shrift of the bread and peanut butter, chewing with relish.

Jennifer pulled up a chair opposite Père Mitya. Every question that had popped into her head in the past few months regarding Alain and Nikki came to mind. They rolled at great speed through her memory bank. Still, the truth was that she didn't know where to start. She was utterly lost in the thicket of questions—until it occurred to her to begin with the one that was uppermost in her mind.

"I want to know about your son," she told him. "I'm in love with Alain. At least, I think I am."

He snorted, and almost choked on his peanut butter.

"My *son*? I can't even teach him how to run a business. He wants to run around the world chasing tail with his tomboy sister. I spoiled my son, Miss Sorel. He was a lonely child with a rather cold mother, so I put him together with his sister. Now I regret that I insisted that they be brought up together. But you never know until it's too late."

"Well, I suppose."

"I suppose you would have known how to deal with two kiddies?" He arched the white fluffy wings above his eyes skeptically. He was touchier than he seemed at first.

"You're the guru."

"I'm not."

"That's what the newspapers say."

"The newspapers have to give quick answers to complicated questions. You look literate, like you can take the hard stuff."

"I'm in love with Alain. That's difficult enough."

"Sure, that's why you're here. That's why I asked you when you walked in my kitchen, what do you want to know?"

"How can I get him to myself—that's what *I* want to know. I thought, you're his father, you might have an idea."

Père Mitya swallowed the last bite of peanut butter and palmed a small belch. He pawed his beard.

"People come to me all the time looking for *ideas*. What do I think about this or that? If I had any grand thoughts of my own, don't you think I'd be out there digging an oil well with my own hands? I can *promise* that you'd see me out there."

Jennifer brushed crumbs into a pile on the table surface near her. "Well, what would you do if you were in my position?"

Père Mitya reached across the white enamel table, his elbow brushing the bread crumbs she'd pushed together. His hands were wrapped around hers as he spoke.

"Jennifer," he said, "my son is a rogue. In fact, he's a wastrel. If I didn't send him a check he would starve."

"Don't you want him to be able to take care of himself?"

"Why should I care what he earns?"

Jennifer thought about this. It was true that Père Mitya's fortune was reputed to be great—and from what she'd seen he supported Alain and Nikki in grand style.

"But don't you care what kind of man he becomes?"

"Of course I do, what do you think? But what can I do? I have to hope for the best."

"What about Nikki?"

"What about her?"

"She sticks to Alain like glue."

"I don't like it, if that's what you're asking. I think they needed to be together at a certain time, when they were children, but now they're grown up."

"*Very* grown up," Jennifer told him.

"Well, they went through my school, my classes, my teachers."

"You were an extraordinary father."

"I was a lousy father. But I think I managed to teach my children what is important. They know not to believe anything they're told, by whatever source, without checking it out for themselves; and they know not to make plans."

"Why did you teach them not to make plans?"

"Because, my dear, plans are for people who are certain there will be a tomorrow."

"Tomorrow seems to keep happening."

"And it will until one day it doesn't. That doesn't mean we should come to count on it."

He beamed and blinked benignly. He had been teasing her by rambling away from her question. He proceeded by indirection to find out what he needed to know, and then offered his advice by the same circuitous route.

"You are a magnificent woman, obviously. You are also intelligent. How did you become involved with my two scamps?"

She told him about seeing Nikki on Fifth Avenue and walking up to her on the terrace at the Stanhope, and then she told him everything else that had happened, up to her experiences in the O group.

He listened carefully, his broad Russian face breaking into laugh lines when she told him some of the more scandalous details.

"Tell me," he asked her when he'd stopped chuckling, "What did you learn from your experiences in quest of the silver pin? You must want it very badly."

"I thought if I earned the silver pin then maybe you would allow me to take pictures of you and some of the people who wear the silver pin. *New Man* magazine would like to do a story, illustrated with my photographs."

His eyes told her nothing of his thoughts. "Yes, go on. Tell me about your experiences. We will put the matter of photographs to one side for a bit."

"I guess the biggest thing I learned is that I didn't know very much about myself sexually."

"Well, humility is always attractive in the young, but can you be a little more specific?"

"I found out who I was. In each situation I saw myself with fresh eyes. I discovered the beauty of my genitals, and I learned how to care for myself sexually. That appealed to me; I like my independence."

"And other people—what did you learn about dealing with them? Did you become more trusting? More open? More natural?"

"Yes. Don't forget that trust was the very first game I played with Nikki. And in O group I was broken, just like your note promised I would be. I was forced to let it all out. You could say that I've been stripped down to my component parts sexually. I am what I am."

He shook his head. "Or, as they say, 'what you see is what you get.' Looking at you, I would be more than happy with that bargain."

"Sex seems horribly complicated at times. It's worth all the fuss, but it *can* be a lot of fuss."

"Yes. That's why I started all this . . . teaching. To try to simplify matters. It seemed to me that everyone was always yammering on and on about sex without knowing *anything* about it—not the slightest thing. Only what their parents taught them, good people who were repeating in turn what *their* parents had taught them. And with every generation the thing got more complicated."

"But the people who wear the silver pin have broken free of their cultural conditioning."

"That's right. When I began teaching about sex as a science—that there were indeed rules for this behavior—I reasoned that there were other people in the world who, like me, knew that sex did not have to be the cause of great guilt, shock, embarrassment, children or matrimony; that it was really a pretty simple affair which would take care of itself quite healthily if left alone. I began to look for these people. Finding them wasn't easy, except in the case of those who had gone public and become sexual performers of one sort or another. I found that people who work in the worlds where flesh is peddled—hookers, porno stars, strippers—were more receptive to my ideas than any other segment of the population. Because they *knew* the truth of it: they worked with the public every day. They saw with their own eyes how a simple human function could be made incredibly complicated."

"What about the people who live here on the ashram with you? I didn't see any silver pins on them."

"Only a few hundred people in the entire world have been given silver pins. They wear the pin so that they may be recognized by others like them. Those who wear the silver pin are sexual masters, capable of performing great services in the cause of Eros. They serve as exemplars to the self-destructive human race, reminders that another kind of world is possible."

"And they've never been together, so they wouldn't recognize each other without the pin?"

"I never see more than one person at a time. Communication is sometimes possible with one person, but never with more than one. The people who live here with me are not adepts. They are simply people who think that my ideas make sense for them, and desire to live together to celebrate this agreement with me. Nice people, but frankly—between you and me—rather dull. You might say that they've taken what I say about sex as a science too literally. They've made it so simple, and so natural, it's lost all its interest. Ironic, isn't it?"

"Frankly, they didn't look very sexy."

"They don't have the fervor it takes to burn with Eros until you're consumed and sex is burnt out of you as clean as white ash."

"Alain said that's how you worked it out. Total celibacy."

"It's a relief for a man who's getting older. Not physically, so much, but emotionally. All the demands made on you by love and jealousy are very exhausting. I've retired from the field, but I like to watch from the sidelines."

Jennifer didn't think she liked the idea.

"I guess I've got a lot of burning left to do, but I hope I never transcend my impulse to open my body to a man's caresses. I need to be touched."

"Amen," he said. While they had talked he had finished the dark bread, eating each piece methodically and with great meditative enjoyment.

Their kitchen conversation had clarified the situation for Jennifer. Talking with Père Mitya confirmed her suspicion that it would be impossible to take pictures of the people around the world who wore the silver pin. It would be not only an intolerable invasion of their privacy, but publicity would very likely ruin the quiet work they did undermining the deadliness of the established order of conventional sex.

But that didn't mean that she couldn't take pictures of Père Mitya, if he would allow her. She hoped he would, because she saw in his Slavic features a character and dignity that she felt uniquely qualified to capture on film.

"Would you let me take pictures of you, Père Mitya? I brought my camera in my bag just in case you agreed to sit for me. It wouldn't take very long."

"I thought you would never ask. I heard the camera bang against the table when you put your bag on it."

He winked at her slyly, lifting his white eyebrows.

"I will not allow you to take pictures of wearers of the silver pin, because it would be counter-productive. People would not understand their work, and there would be sensational headlines. But you can snap me if you want. I've watched your eyes and I think you will take very good pictures."

Jennifer felt so excited she wanted to jump across the table and kiss Père Mitya. She took the camera from her bag and put it up to her eye, looking for focus and exposure.

"Don't pose," she told him. "Just sit there at the table brushing the crumbs."

Père Mitya was one man across a kitchen table and quite another in the lens of a camera. Through the camera his large hooked nose told a story beyond words. The swirls and Rococo splendors of his white beard were the punctuation of his personality. The benign eyes became fiery through the lens. The camera transformed him beautifully when it found the revolutionary in the self-effacing man whose teachings about the simplicity of sexuality—the application of scientific principles to counteract cultural conditioning—had spread its good news through the world.

Père Mitya was a ham. His smile was beautiful and radiant, his eyes were full of love. Seldom had Jennifer photographed a man whose face so well expressed the truth of his personality. This was a man whose very *being* was photogenic.

When she had finished the third roll of film she put her camera down and called enough. "I could go on snapping the shutter all night," she told him. "Your face goes through so many changes."

"Enough. Thank you," he said, waving his hand. "This is exhausting." Both elbows were propped on the table.

"You were a ham."

"Oh? You think I'm vain?" He cocked his head. "That tickles me. Perhaps I am. . . ." He plucked dreamily for a moment at his beard.

She could see that he was getting tired. It was late, time to wind up her visit with him. She realized that she had spent more time with Père Mitya than most of his disciples were ever allowed, and the one question uppermost in her mind had not been answered.

She asked it directly, standing in the kitchen looking at the white bearded man sitting heavily at the enamel kitchen table. So far he had circumnavigated her question.

"What should I do about Alain? I'm in love with him, but Nikki hangs about him like a ghost. I won't be a third in a relationship."

"No, you shouldn't. It's time for Alain and Nikki to go their separate ways romantically. Their closeness was all right when they were younger, but they've taken it too far."

"Do you have any ideas you want to share with me on how to separate them?"

"Just one: distraction. The only reason Nikki has stayed so close to Alain is that she's never met any man to equal him."

"That is pretty hard to do. Despite his faults, Alain is one of a kind."

"Introduce my daughter to a man. She's the right age."

Jennifer frowned, unable to think of such a man right off the bat. Nikki knew that she had the best in her own brother: he had looks, intelligence, sexual experience, daring, and a comforting sense of the absurd.

"It's time for you to go now," he told her. "Having a woman of your beauty alone in my house starts the old bells ringing, so get out of here."

"All right," she agreed, gathering up her things and putting on her coat. "You are right. It's time."

She approached him to say good-bye, reaching out for his comforting arms in the dimly lighted kitchen. When he embraced her, she felt reassured about everything.

She stepped away and he said, "Don't go yet," so she stood waiting for him at the table. She had an idea of what he was fumbling for in the pockets of his rough jacket.

He came up with it at last, like a child brandishing a lighted firecracker. It was a tiny silver pin in the shape of an O.

"You wear this, to remind people that there *is* an alternative."

# 21

It was St. Valentine's Day, one day before Lupercalia, the ancient Roman fertility festival celebrated on February fifteenth by wearers of the silver pin. Yuri Muscovy was making his final American appearance in "Swan Lake", before going on an extended European tour. The black tie ballet crowd was lined up to get in. On the great plaza outside the theater scalpers did a brisk business.

Jennifer knew that it would be her last chance to see Yuri. She called him and explained that she would like to bring her friend Nikki Armitage backstage to meet him after the performance.

"Yes, yes," he'd said, "but I hope we can get rid of her. I want to spend some time with you."

When Jennifer and Nikki walked into the lobby of the theater that evening there was a lull in the buzz of conversation as people turned to notice the two most beautiful women of the evening.

They swept into the lobby arm in arm, Jennifer in the ermine coat Yuri had given her, her blonde hair set in golden ringlets so that she looked like a Greek goddess; and dark, exotic-looking Nikki swathed from ankle to neck in white marabou fur.

They settled back in their seats and the house lights dimmed. The wonderful romantic Tchaikovsky music washed over them. When Yuri Muscovy appeared on stage the familiar movements were given a new poetic dimension. Jennifer and Nikki did not take their eyes from him all the time he was on stage.

"He's gorgeous," Nikki breathed at intermission.

"Would you like to meet him?" Jennifer asked. She didn't feel in the least guilty for having manipulated Nikki to this point.

"Jennifer, he's a god! I would give anything to meet him!"

When the curtain fell, Nikki sat back and took a deep breath.

"I have seen something tonight that I never expected to see in my lifetime: Absolute beauty wedded to absolute grace. I'd be happy forever if I could share a few minutes with a man like Yuri Muscovy."

Nikki was being typically excessive, but Jennifer was convinced that seeing Yuri was going to change Nikki's life. She hoped it would.

When the applause had died down, after the fifth curtain call, Jennifer took Nikki backstage, using the passes Yuri had left for her to get to his private dressing room.

Yuri was striding back and forth dressed in a velvet robe when they entered. His high forehead still glowed from the effort of the dance. He was feeling rapturous after his performance, a temporary euphoria that was all the more poignant because it was transitory.

"This always stirs my soul. Tchaikovsky wrote profoundly Russian music. I weep for my homeland when I hear it."

"You were wonderful, Yuri," Jennifer said. "I brought a friend of mine to meet you. She was very moved by your performance. This is Nikki Armitage."

Yuri bowed dramatically and bent over Nikki's hand. Her dark eyes welled over with pleasure. It was the first time Jennifer could remember seeing Nikki struck speechless.

"Did you like the music?" he inquired.

"I didn't hear the music."

"You didn't *hear* Tchaikovsky?"

"I was watching you. There was no time to listen."

"Oh," he said, flashing his strong white teeth. "That's different." His broad, craggy face broke into a pleased smile.

"You were a god up there."

"Yes, I suppose I was good. Perhaps I might have slowed things just a fraction. . . ."

It was a test. He watched her with lifted eyebrows.

"Well, yes," Nikki said tentatively. "It might have added a more poetic dimension. . . .

"On the other hand, your performance might have lost some of its animal vigor."

Jennifer watched the surprised pleasure in Yuri's eyes. He was hooked. She had to admire the efficiency with which Nikki worked. Yuri had not had a chance.

"You seem to be very discerning about dance, Miss Armitage."

"Nikki. Just Nikki. I am your slave. From this day I am going to devote myself to you."

"But surely you're out of your mind." He looked to Jennifer for confirmation. "I don't understand American women. Jennifer, you promised to explain them to me."

Jennifer shrugged. "Every woman has a secret fantasy mate that she may or may not know about consciously, but when she sees him she recognizes him immediately. I think Nikki recognized you the minute she saw you. I was sitting next to her, and I saw her response to you."

Yuri looked thoughtful, impressed but uncertain how to proceed. He scratched his head and paced back and forth in front of the two women.

He noticed that they were both still wearing their coats, and it was very hot in the dressing room.

"Take off your coats. Take off your coats and we will have some champagne. I am celebrating tonight."

"Are you happy about going to Europe?"

"Yes. I understand the women there. They don't make such pronouncements."

A bottle of chilled champagne sat in a silver ice bucket on his dressing table, which was lighted by dozens of little bulbs. Stuck among them were congratulatory telegrams.

"Drink, drink," he urged them, pouring the bubbly wine into glasses and handing them to the two women, who had put their coats on a chair.

Jennifer wore a black tissue faille dress illuminated with silver sequins—and set among them, her silver pin. Nikki looked ultra-feminine in a lace blouse with a black satin sash at the waist and a long black skirt.

"You are both so beautiful that I don't know how

to salute you properly. How does a mere man behave with nymphs?"

"He makes love to them if he wants to. He takes them as a king or a god might. He takes them because his art and beauty have bestowed such gifts as rewards for his talents."

Nikki told him this while effortlessly holding his attention with her sparkling dark eyes. It was as if she were telling him a fairy tale. His voice was thick when he answered her.

"Dancing is very sexual. You were stimulated by that. Do you imagine that I am the same man off stage? Jennifer knows that I am not."

Nikki smiled as if to say she was not Jennifer. She would look at him with fire in her eyes no matter what he said to her. Jennifer recognized the stubbornness in Nikki's expression. She saw something that she wanted, and she was going to have it.

The success of Jennifer's plan depended upon Nikki getting what she wanted, and Jennifer was determined to help her any way she could.

"Yuri," she said. "I have to warn you. Nikki is accustomed to having her own way. There's no use putting up resistance."

Yuri nodded and glared at Nikki, his face dark.

"You are spoiled, like most American women," he accused her.

"That's true."

"You want to make love to me?"

"That's what I said."

"Right here? With Jennifer in the room?"

"I'm used to having what I want without waiting for it."

"Bah! How do I know what to think? It's crazy to walk into a man's dressing room and offer to make love to him just like that. I think it is very brazen."

"I *am* very brazen. Ask Jennifer."

Yuri swallowed the last drop of his third glass of champagne. which clearly was going to his head. Nikki's calm replies to his questions left him with nowhere to turn. Jennifer saw the lust creep into his florid face like the shadows of dusk.

"Will you do anything for me?" he asked Nikki. "Anything?"

"Just ask me."

"Show me your breasts. Open your blouse so that I can see them. I think they must be very small and shy."

Nikki smiled at her victory, and opened the first two buttons of her lace blouse. The dark beauty of her exotic features contrasted strongly with the white lace."

"Why are you stopping?" he asked.

"I thought you might want to open the rest of the buttons."

"Yes, I will open them." His fingers fumbled over the tiny buttons, his palms sliding over Nikki's small, firm breasts. Jennifer saw Nikki's nipples sticking through the blouse. When Yuri had opened it to the velvet waistband, he stuck his hand inside and squeezed both handfuls of flesh.

"I wish they were bigger for you," Nikki gasped apologetically, her face tightening with the pleasure his hands were giving her.

Jennifer felt like an intruder as she watched this passionate interplay. She waited for an opening where she might step in and help Nikki to her goal.

"Does it feel good to touch them, Yuri? Feel how my nipples are getting hard? The same thing is happening all over my body. I want you to know that it's only for you, that I've been wet since I saw you come on stage tonight. It was like you were dancing for me alone, making love to me alone. I couldn't take my eyes off the bulge in your tights."

## Book Five

His eyes were wide with shock and pleasure. He was obviously stimulated by her words, but just as obviously couldn't quite believe what he heard.

"You are so bold," he said wonderingly. "In Russia a woman would never talk like this."

"I can't wait any longer, Yuri. I know you're hard, I can see it through your robe. I know you're excited."

"Oh, you American wonder!" Yuri cried, opening the sash of his robe and displaying his powerful erection. It stood up from the center of his powerful dancer's body like a sapling.

"You have got me so excited," Yuri said. "Look at what you've created—this monster who must have his own way." He smacked his stiff flesh with both hands, as if punishing it for being so single-minded.

Nikki sank to her knees before Yuri and knelt not far from the tip of his penis, breathing warmly on it.

"This is what I want," she said as if in a trance. "Oh, how I want this." She looked up at Jennifer without a trace of embarrassment. "Help me, Jennifer. Hold him steady for me."

Jennifer didn't understand at first. What did she mean? But she stood behind the transfixed Yuri, and reached around his body to grip his thick penis at the base, holding it straight out and steady for the magic Nikki was working on it from in front.

Like a snake-charmer, Nikki approached Yuri's swollen knob with her lips and stuck her tongue out —the tip just touching the coronal rim. She flickered her tongue, touching it to the opening from which a pearly drop of pre-coital fluid had leaked. Yuri moved his body forward involuntarily to get closer to her mouth, but each time she moved back, keeping him at bay while she teased him wickedly.

"I must have you now," he grunted. "I can't stand

any more of this. If you don't stop I will splash all over your face."

"No you won't, not yet. I'm going to show you how to prolong this a little longer. . . ."

"Do you want to drive me crazy?"

"Yes, that's the idea."

She stood up, ignoring his throbbing erection, and walked to his dressing table.

"I've always wondered what it would be like to be taken on a table," she said. "I'm going to find out right now."

She hopped up on the table and pulled her black skirt up over her black stockings. She was wearing a garter belt that framed her naked hairless sex with black lace.

"I'm wide open for you, Yuri. I want you so much my stomach is going crazy. My heart is beating like a trip hammer. Come over here and fuck me."

Yuri crossed the small room in a trance, totally at Nikki's mercy, his erection stabbing the air before him.

Nikki held up her arms, pulling his body to her, wrapping her legs around him, so that all Jennifer saw was her black stockings crossed around Yuri's back. She stepped closer, excited now herself. The dancer's large, muscular buttocks thrust and flexed, thrust and flexed, making dimples in the hollows. She stepped closer and caressed them, running her hand into his crease and pushing him into Nikki.

"Oh," he cried. "I don't believe this is happening!"

"More, Yuri. Push yourself into me with all your might. Hurry now, before I come. Hurry, hurry. . . ."

Her legs loosened around his back and he grasped them firmly and put them over his shoulders so that he could thrust more deeply into Nikki.

"Now, Yuri. Now, come with me!" she cried.

"Wait, wait, let me catch up to you, you're so fast!" he grunted explosively between his teeth.

"Oh, that's good. I'm coming I think. Oh yes, there it is—can you feel it? Can you feel it, Yuri?"

"It's fluttering, like a bird. I can feel it!" he shouted. "Oh you're doing me in! You're doing me in!"

They were lost in each other, in the alternate world they had created so spontaneously. Jennifer smiled and shook her head. Nikki had surprised her again.

They were no longer aware that she was in the room. She walked quietly to her coat and put it on, and tiptoed out of the room, leaving them to their erotic *pas de deux*.

Nikki called her several days later with the news.

"You won't believe what I'm going to do, Jennifer."

"Try me. You taught me about surprises, remember?"

"I'm going with Yuri on his European tour. He says now that he's met me, he won't be able to dance unless I'm there every night."

"Congratulations."

"I'm just worried about Alain, what he'll do without me."

"Oh, I think he'll manage. Don't worry, Nikki."

"Would you do me a favor, Jennifer?"

"Sure."

"Would you take care of him for me? He needs looking after."

Nikki couldn't see the grin on Jennifer's face when she answered. "Sure, Nikki, I'll look after him. Nothing would make me happier."

# 22

For sun-drenched days without end they followed the green Tobago coast on the yacht *Silver Eagle*, a sleek eighty foot boat that was made for speed and adventure. In the evenings they'd find a berth in some cove and cook the fish they'd caught, and they'd make love. They made love night and day and got nut-brown in the Caribbean sun.

They were scudding in a fine breeze against a blue horizon. Jennifer lay prone on the deck, sunbathing and day-dreaming. She was a vision of blondeness from her sunbleached hair down her dark and glowing body. She wore only a tiny black bikini that was more provocation than covering. It provided unnecessary emphasis to her rounded buttocks and shapely thighs.

She had been trying to write in her journal for days, but happiness was hard to write about. At least the kind of happiness she had realized with Alain was impossible for her to write about. Instead she recorded the impressions that drifted and darted through her mind like dolphins playing in the emerald depths.

She wrote in a large, dramatic hand.

*This is heaven, but heaven can't be so watery, so smooth, so gliding. And yet it is: When I pinch myself I'm still here, still sunning myself in the middle of an ancient sea. The boat moves on, skipping like a stone on the water.*

*Alain is a different man by himself. Without his sister he is calm, imperturbable. When we make love he is tireless. Sometimes I have to beg him to stop. He seems now less the arrogant young man, more the satisfied sensualist who has come to terms with things.*

*Nikki and Yuri are off in Europe. We had a postcard from the Netherlands, but that was weeks ago, when we put into port to pick up mail and supplies. She is still wildly infatuated, and Alain says that is her nature, that she will remain that way. He seems not to think of her, although I can't be sure when he gets that faraway look in his eyes what he's remembering.*

*Now that I've got the silver pin he treats me with new respect. I don't think he believed that his father would give me the pin. He looks at me sometimes like he's wondering what kind of magic powers I have.*

*I've invited Marina down to the island for*

*next month. She needs a reason to escape Jack August, and I think I owe her, after she went to bat for me with Jack. Jack is upset because I decided not to do the pictures of Père Mitya's followers. I tried to explain to him that the public wouldn't understand what Père Mitya was up to, but he wouldn't listen to that. I gave him the pictures I took of Père Mitya and he was only slightly mollified.*

*I'm afraid my poor dear sister took the brunt of Jack's displeasure with me. It's time for her to say farewell to him, I think.*

She stopped writing and looked up at the midday sun. She expected any minute to be joined on the deck by Alain, who spent this time every day discussing their cruise plans with the skipper of the *Silver Eagle*. In addition to the finest Chinese cook in Jamaica, the boat carried three crewmen who ran the boat smoothly and efficiently.

She looked up and smiled when she heard his footsteps.

"How'd you like to go snorkeling, darling?" he asked. "Skipper says we're coming up on a good spot." He pointed over the side to the clear aquamarine depths. "There's coral down there."

"Never mind coral. Come here."

"Yes?" He took a step toward her.

"Come closer, silly."

He leaned over her, propped on his spread fingers, and she put her arms around his neck.

"Right here. Right on the deck," she said.

He looked around. "What about the crew?"

"What about them?"

"Well, they're all over the place. They'll notice."

"I don't care. They know what we're doing down in our cabin every morning and evening and some-

## Book Five

times in the afternoon when we're in the shower. They should be pretty broad-minded by now. If I learned anything earning the silver pin, it's not to be embarrassed by onlookers."

She ran the tips of her fingers lightly over the prominent bulge in his blue French briefs. She pulled the elastic waistband and his penis sprang out, fully erect.

"Oh, my. Look at *that*. I want to feel it inside me. I want to have it right this minute. It's so big and hard, and look how red it's getting. That's not sun burn!"

He chuckled at her language, but he knew she was serious.

"Come on, just get on top of me. Do it from behind—it's more exciting that way. More convenient, too. Look, I'll put my ass up in the air and wiggle it for you."

He helped her pull the black bikini bottoms down her curved, taut thighs, but they got caught around her ankle. He looked down at the satisfying sight of her round rump—a startling white next to the copper color of her tan—and at the two openings that invited his attention. They winked and glistened at him.

He gripped his stiff penis at the base and moved forward on his knees to place it in her vagina. He **pushed into her slowly, feeling the tight suction along** the length of his hardness like small lips nibbling at him. When he'd sunk all the way into her tight crevice an insane pleasure gripped him and he pushed in and out as rapidly as he could, trying to maintain the delirious level of sensation.

"That's it, Alain. Just keep doing that forever, darling. Oh my wonderful lover, you know how to use it, you know how to use it. . . ."

She squirmed under his weight and moved her

ass against him, into his thrusts. Both of them were oblivious to the sun above, the sea below them, the eyes that watched them.

His belly cleaved to her bridging back, as she supported herself on hands and knees while he reached around her body to cup her breasts in his hands. They were full and firm and the nipples butted softly into his palms.

"Jennifer, it feels like I'm going to get lost in you and never come to the surface, like I'm being pulled into a whirlpool."

"Let yourself be pulled, Alain, don't resist it. Fuck me, put yourself into my ass, do anything. . . ."

He moved, slipping out of her vagina and up into her winking anus, finding no more resistance there than he'd found in her cunt. He entered gently, but once inside the same fever possessed him and he again thrust into her with as much energy as he could summon. He felt he was on the verge of a major explosion when she suddenly stopped moving her hips and slipped out from under him. She sat up.

"I want you to play a game with me," she said mischievously, aware of the havoc she had caused by disconnecting from him. "Will you?"

"Anything, my darling. Anything you want. Just tell me."

She twisted her splendid brown body and reached for the tiny black top of her bikini that had been tossed on the deck in his eagerness to caress her breasts.

"Come here," she commanded. Puzzled, he moved closer. Quickly she tied the top of her bikini around his eyes. The sunlight and the sea was shut out in an instant, and his hands reached for empty air when he tried to embrace her.

"Just trust me, Alain," she said. "Now it's my turn to drive *you* crazy."